Five of a Feather

a fable

Angela Jeffs

Angela Jeffs

Website: **www.angelajeffs.co.uk**
Author page: **https://www.facebook.com/epicbooks4U/**
Twitter: **Angela Jeffs @jeffs_angela**

First edition 2020

ISBN-13: 978-1974389858 (KDP-Assigned)
ISNB-10: 1974389855

BISAC – Fable/fiction

Published by KDP (Kindle Direct Publishing). Paperback printed to order or available on Kindle via Amazon.com

For Maxford,
who has always loved a good story.

&

In memory of dancer-choreographer Nikolas Dixon (1956-2018), artist/writer/poet Tony Rickaby (1944-2018), and translator Geraldine Harcourt (1952-2019), who were all magnificent storytellers in their own unique ways.

You know those ducks in that pond right near Central Park South? That little lake? By any chance, do you happen to know where they go, the ducks, when it all gets frozen over? Do you happen to know by any chance?

J. D. SALINGER (THE CATCHER IN THE RYE)

Fallen leaves return to the root.

CHINESE PROVERB

Contents

Prologue

I must thank neighbours here in Forneth for the original inspiration for this story. It all happened as written, except that apparently I was told the ducks were ducks, and the idea that they were Mandarins and in any way connected to China was simply a product of my own Oriental-orientated imaginings.

Also I must apologise to all creatures great and small for putting human words into mouths and beaks. I am not a fan of anthropomorphism, that is, giving animals the human characteristics of speech and/or behaviour. In this case I have tried to find an acceptable middle ground: that is, the humans communicate with one another, and ditto the birds, but neither humans nor birds 'talk' to one another.

As to my main characters, based on the nine personality types of the Enneagram, a centuries-old spiritual and psychological system, I love them all, for their flaws and courage and willingness to change and thus, by a slow but steady process of integration, find balance, peace and reinvention in their lives.

THE CAST OF NINE (in order of appearance)

Challenger 8
CONG (great)
Perfectionist 1
DEWEI (great principle)
Loyalist 6
SHUANG (bright, clear and open-hearted)
Helper 2
HU-TU (earth mother)
Peacemaker 9
BO (precious)

Sceptic 5
CHUNG (wise one)

Epicure 7
LOK (happy)
Performer 3
LI QIN (beautiful [stringed] musical instrument)

Artist 4
CHII-NII (goddess of spinners, weavers and dreams)

Scotland

Ye see yon quackin', spune-faced bird,
Wi' wabbit feet an' a' that,
That waddles gravely through the yird?
It's but a deuk for a' that.
For a' that an' a' that,
Its gracefu' neck an' a' that,
Though it can soom whaur hens wad droon,
A hen's a hen for a' that.

Anon.
(A parody of Robert Burns' poem, "A Man's a Man for a' That", seeming to admire the birds rather than humankind)

(You see that quacking spoon-faced bird,
With webbed feet and all that,
That waddles gravely through the yard?
It's but a duck for all that,
For all that and all that,
Its graceful neck and all that,
Though it can swim where hens would drown,
A hen's a hen for all that.)

The five young ducks came with the promise of snow and not much more.

They came out of the cold in a cardboard box, carried with a singular lack of care and not a hint of apology by a complete stranger to the house: a large red-faced man in a kilt and trainers.

They were no ordinary ducks, the rude, unexpected guest announced, forgetting their age and dumping the box on the kitchen floor in order to lift the back of his kilt to warm his backside at the Aga stove.

He was a Sassenach really but had made enough money to play at being a Scottish landowner. The woman, who, unlike her somewhere below the borders-born husband really was a homemaking Highlander, knew this immediately because the rude, unexpected guest was wearing boxer shorts under custom-designed tartan, which no self-respecting clansman would surely ever do.

They were Chinese ducks, whatever that meant, the rude, unexpected guest continued, assuming his audience to be as unconscious as he was. Anyway, he was just not a duck person, and without a word of thanks accepted a mug of what he assumed to be steaming straight tea.

Knowing little to nothing about Chinese ducks themselves, the somewhere below the borders-born man and his homemaking Highland wife didn't know what to say. But being naturally kind – and by upbringing polite – they asked how he had come by them.

Oh dear.

It seemed that the rude, unexpected guest's silly wife had seen them in a pet shop in Glasgow and thought them cute. But all they did was dirty the lawn, mess up her pond, and try to eat her shag pile carpet.

He had taken them on because he thought they were the same

as the Peking Duck you could eat in Chinese restaurants and would taste good. But as he had learned to his cost, they didn't.

The somewhere below the borders-born man and the homemaking Highland woman looked at one another. Did this mean that there were now fewer birds than when he'd first bought them?

Oh double dear ...

As to communication, the rude, unexpected guest prattled on (madly in love with the sound of his own booming voice), just an endless stream of what sounded like cluck clucks and quack quacks ... not exactly a huge vocabulary.

Nor, he added darkly, did they do anything.

Hens laid eggs. Dogs did as they were told. Horses could win fortunes on the hoof, chase foxes under the whip, fetch a good price for stud.

But Chinese ducks or whatever they were? Useless ... a complete waste of time and space. Why didn't they just fly away and save everyone a lot of trouble? Isn't that what ducks are normally supposed to do? Fly?

Really, thought the couple (but were too kind to say so), how truly ignorant and resultingly unpleasant can some people be.

And their hearts went out to the five little birds, maybe too old to be called ducklings but still young and adolescent, huddled quietly at the bottom of the box, three brightly coloured and two less so, one of which appeared to have a damaged wing.

Just yesterday, the rude, unexpected guest yapped on, his silly wife had decided that ducks were boring and far too much trouble. Instead she was thinking of ordering a plastic swan from some catalogue. At least that could be scrubbed and would stay still.

Anyway, he had asked around for help, and the all-knowing, all-seeing groundsman at the golf club had suggested his Good Life neighbours who, as God-fearing folk and as Green as they come, would surely take them in.

As soon as he had completed his eighteen holes, the rude, unexpected guest had belted home and eaten dinner – chicken stovie from the deep freeze.

Then he'd got his dog to round up the birds, shoved them in a box and – without even resorting to the convenience of his smartphone to warn of his arrival – driven them across the valley to where the Good Life couple lived high above the loch, with a large pond, a gaggle of geese, a flock of hens and a roof of solar panels.

Och aye, I'll be awae then, he said, affecting (badly) a pseudo-Scottish accent and putting down the cup of herb tea he had been offered, courtesy of a souvenir gift pack from Istanbul. Relieved that the problem was no longer his own, he was even more relieved that he could escape a drink that tasted (to him) like compost.

Foreign muck, he nearly said, but managed to swallow the words instead, along with a clove that stuck in his throat and made him choke all the way home.

Well! agreed the somewhere below the borders-born man and the homemaking Highland woman, who were so close after forty years that they often expressed the same thought at the same time.

That quite takes the biscuit, she continued, watching the tail light of the SUV disappear into the night. And then she laughed, because she had quite forgotten to offer him one: a homemade oatmeal flapjack.

So yes, the ducks – Chinese Mandarins – were unexpected but of course very welcome, they agreed. After all, none of this human behaviour was their fault. The creatures were, they supposed, simply victims of their unique prettiness.

But what to do with them?

Too late to put them in the field with the geese, said the somewhere below the borders-born man, who was not only a sustainable tree planter but also a dyker, meaning he liked to spend any remaining spare time rebuilding stone walls.

Too late to introduce them to the pond, agreed his homemaking Highland wife, tentatively introducing a forefinger into the box and stroking the smallest drab-coloured bird, which shivered and made a small sound that was immediately picked up by the others and set them all a-quiver.

Poor little things, she said. They're terrified.

And she packed some of the raw fleece she was preparing to spin to weave into a blanket into the corners of the box, to help keep them warm.

I'll put them in the log house for the night, her husband decided. They should be safe in there. We'll think about what to do next in the morning.

So saying, he picked up the box, carried it outside and opened the log house door. He made a space a few feet off the floor, just in case of foxes, and laid the box carefully in place.

See you tomorrow, little ones, the somewhere below the borders-born man said softly. And closed the door behind him.

IN FEAR AND TREMBLING

The birds huddled against one another in fear and trembling. The darkness was intense. So was their hunger. The human had put a bowl of water just outside the box, and though they could not see it, they could smell it.

So first they clambered out, cleverly climbing one on top of another but more by instinct than design, and helping the weakest go first. Then they found the water and lapped and lapped until it was all gone.

Now what?

Follow the leader, except they had no leader ... despite being siblings they were not even aware that one must have broken out of its shell ahead of the others. So they did what most ducks do in moments of stress or indecision: put their heads under their wings and slept.

GONE!

The snow came in the darkness of early morning. Not heavily, but enough to alter the rolling landscape, softening its outlines and scattering the ground with feather-like patches of white.

By the time the somewhere below the borders-born man and homemaking Highland woman had climbed out from under their duvet, dressed, listened to the news on the BBC's Radio 4 and made breakfast, it was nearly 9am.

The ducks, she remembered.

I'll check, bring them in, said her husband.

But when he opened the log house door and checked the box, it was empty.

The Mandarins had gone.

THE GREAT ESCAPE

The five siblings had gone looking for food. As dawn allowed them to identify spaces between planks and holes in corners as escape routes, they had crept out into another strange world.

Snow flakes were drifting down in a desultory manner, as if undecided whether to turn serious or not.

The ducks began to peck the ground, looking for anything edible. But insects were in short supply; they were all in hiding. It was the bird table that saved them, the base littered with seeds and nuts, thrown to the ground by the greedy careless beaks of wild feathered compatriots.

They ate until the last unfamiliar pulse and grain had gone, and then began to waddle away from the house, following the wall that best offered protection, which unbeknownst to them led down to the road. They could hear geese honking down near the pond but, though drawn to the water and overhanging trees, felt insecure. The noise sounded aggressive, unfriendly; best not to go there.

The three males, with their beautiful developing plumage, led the way, followed by the healthy female and her wounded sister limping at the rear – or rather dragging her injured wing along the ground.

It was tough going. Grasses were stiff with ice; stones slippery. It was not easy terrain to navigate even in early winter.

Do we know what we're doing? murmered one of those in the lead to a brother.

Not a clue, came the reply.

But is it a good idea?

Dunno. Just keep going.

Keep going where?

Wherever we're going …

Which concluded that first relatively conscious conversation with a surprisingly philosophical twist.

When they reached the road, they found a ruined wall awaiting restoration (one that the below the borders-born dyker had not yet got around to) and huddled back together in a cleft between several boulders. Sleep came easy again; full stomachs always had that effect on them.

VANISHED INTO THIN AIR?

The homemaking Highland woman was extremely upset. She could not understand how the birds had got out, or where they could possibly have gone.

They must be so cold, so hungry, she worried, tears in her eyes.

We have to go and look for them.

So she and her husband put on boots and coats and hats and scarves and gloves and went outside.

First they looked into and around the log house. True, there were some holes in the walls, but big enough for ducks?

The strange thing was there were no webprints in the snow, no indication as to which way (having escaped) they might gone.

I'm guessing the snow came after, covering up any trail, said the man. Let's go look in the field.

So they walked around their field, and the field next door that was owned by a neighbour further up the hill. Then they walked down the lane to the main road, but still there was no sign, no hint, not a single clue.

It's as if they've vanished into thin air, observed the woman, nonplussed. Are we sure we didn't dream the whole thing?

No, the box is there, complete with their droppings. And as for what's his name, the idiot who brought them, he was no dream. He was a nightmare.'

His wife gave him a look and then laughed.

Back in the house they knelt down and, being Christian, prayed that the ducks would be okay wherever they were, and were sure that even if they were dead they would have gone to heaven.

At which point the clock chimed 11am and coffee time. To which they both said Amen.

SOUTH SOUNDS LIKE A GOOD WORD

When the ducks woke, the winter sun was dazzling. They blinked, tried to remember where they were and why, but failed miserably, so blinked again.

Hearing sounds, they poked their heads out and found they were looking directly across the road – a wider stretch of black and white with patches of tar and melting snow – to a box on wheels, out of which music was playing. There was the sound of whistling too, a sound they were more in tune with, but where was it coming from?

From a human male with dark hair and a salt and pepper beard, climbing up a pole.

What was he doing, this bearded middle-aged man? Fiddling about with wires and cables, with some kind of harness looped and hooked around his body.

Is he making magic? asked the healthy female duck.

What's magic? asked her sister, trying to find a position that was comfortable. Her wing did not hurt, but it was irritating the way it failed to work properly.

I suspect it is magic that has got us this far, answered the male duck that had led the way down to the road. So maybe it is magic that got the middle-aged human up so high without wings.

Ah ha, they clucked gently in appreciation of yet another seemingly clever thought.

Hungry again, they crept out of the back of the pile of stones and found themselves close to the lower part of the pond they had avoided during the night. With no signs of life, barring a few half-frozen snails in the swampy sedge – the geese were up near the house, by the sound of it, demanding breakfast with a barrage of hoots and honks – they paddled tentatively through the slushy mud to skim the surface to feed. Only the small injured female clung to land, unsure of her balance in water.

Hearing the music stop, they returned to see that the bearded middle-aged man had climbed down and was eating something in the front seat of his box on wheels.

A sandwich, declared the healthy female. I have seen them before. They were all that the female human who said we were dirty ever made for her young ones. I could never understand why when her kitchen was so shiny. The shiniest kitchen I have ever seen.

And how many have you seen? teased the second male duck who unlike his brothers had kept pretty quiet until now. Expert, are you?

Two, she replied stoutly. And it was the shiniest yet.

She had, she realized, missed out on the kitchen the night before. In the box, she could see little, but there had been a good feeling about it, and the smells were interesting if not shiny – wood smoke, baking, wet washing drying, herbs ...

So never mind. There would be more, she supposed. After all, where there were humans, there were places to prepare food. That was one of the many odd things about humans. They had to mess around with food and make it different. In that respect she thought ducks were much more sensible; all they had to do was snap up a beak full of worms and slither, sliver, down it all went.

Excuse me, interrupted the third male, who was being suitably polite to his elder brothers and helpful all round. There's another box on wheels coming ...

This time the vehicle, with the same markings on its sides as the other, but pointing in the opposite direction, stopped on their side of the road. Hallo there, Sandy. Been having your lunch then?

Aye, Angus. Where are you off to?

Edinburgh, if the snow doesn't get worse.

Are there holdups on the A9?

Aye, a few, but only ben to Inverness. Not down south.

The duck who had taken the lead sat up. South. This sounded like a good word. Or at least warmer.

The new man who had no face (because he was wearing a mask against the cold and his hat pulled low) quickly began opening the back of his van, and lowering some kind of ramp.

I've got the equipment you need, Sandy. Shall I bring it over?

Aye, Angus, I'd appreciate that.

And the man who had no face was soon wheeling something large and noisy across the road out of sight behind the other side of the first vehicle.

Follow me, ordered the drake who was once again seizing the day. And be quick. Or as quick as you can ...

The female with the damaged wing gathered together all her strength and determination and began to drag herself after the others. The males left her to it but her sister fussed around in motherly fashion, making sure she did not get left behind.

They waddled around the back of the van and up the ramp, and on into the furthest darkest recesses of the interior, filled as it was with machinery and telecommunications-related bits and pieces.

I'm not sure about this, said the third male, who felt both excited and terrified at the same time.

Nor am I, agreed the female with the damaged wing, who was exhausted and scared all over again.

The duck who had taken the lead was not one hundred per cent sure either, but he had heard the word south. And without really knowing what it meant, knew instinctively that it was the way they had to go.

ANOTHER STRANGE PLACE

They bounced and bumped and slid for ages, until the van came to a halt and the man with no face opened up the back, took out a bag of some kind and disappeared.

Where are we?

What shall we do?

Follow me!

They had to jump off the back because the ramp was not down. When it came to the female with the damaged wing, her healthier sister helped break her fall in a feathery flutter.

Where shall we go?

What shall we do?

Follow me!

And so they played follow the leader yet again into a dark corner of an alley, with overflowing dustbins, piles of rubbish, an old car, and dubious-looking back exits of offices and cafes and clubs.

Where are we? asked the healthy female.

I think it must be Edinburgh, though I had heard it was a castle, not a slum, replied the duck who was now, in all but rational understanding, in charge.

What's a castle? asked one sibling.

What's a slum? asked another.

The duck who was now leader in all but name was silent. He hadn't a clue. He'd heard things sometimes and remembered things vaguely, but that was all. He knew nothing. And, worst of all, he was beginning to realise that he knew nothing.

The two things he was good at, though, the others agreed, was looking after them all and taking the initiative. Which in the circumstances was very useful.

Imagine where we'd still be if you had not said do this, do that, remarked the third male, who admired his charismatic brother while resisting his being so organized.

Maybe in a better place than this, sniped the second male, who felt he would be a better leader but found it easier to criticise than challenge.

But they all shivered at the thought of that dreadful pond that smelled of chemicals, the ignorant, thoughtless man and woman who had reduced them from seven to five, and the dreadful dog that, in bullying them out of the water and into the box, had all but snapped their heads off.

They shivered even harder when thinking back to the cage in the pet shop, which was so hard on their webbed feet, and the humiliation and stress that all the birds and animals suffered as they waited to be purchased.

Before that the ducks could hardly remember ... only something ... something warm and safe, and then...terror, and darkness, and then bright lights that hurt their eyes, and unfamiliar food and dirty water that made them feel sick.

Now they were in another strange place, feeling cold and damp (the snow had turned to sleet) and nauseous with fear all over again. But, as the duck who was leader said soothingly, at least they were together.

I'm going to find the best place to hide, he said decisively. And waddled off between the bins and rubbish until he found an old torn blanket lying on the ground under the back of the even older car, and scrambled underneath, calling for the others to join him.

The alley was not a nice place. It felt threatening and smelled disgusting.

Sometimes doors opened and various humans came out, urinating into the rubbish or puffing smoke. The dreadful people – the rude man and his foolish wife – had puffed smoke too, but this aroma was different, quite pleasant in fact. Soothed even further, the ducks napped, drank from dirty puddles of snow melt and waited … waited for hour after hour for something to happen. Which, life being as it is, eventually did.

RESCUE

Just after midnight, the door opened and a young male human with pink hair and the suggestion of extensive tattoos around his wrists came out carrying an oddly shaped box on a strap over his shoulder. He stopped at the back of the car and opened up the boot, the sound of which woke the ducks and set them all a-flutter.

What the hell … said the young man with pink hair, and kicked back the filthy blanket at his feet while at the same time swearing at the passing tramp he supposed had left it there.

What the … he mouthed, as he and the ducks met eye to eye. He could not have been more astonished if they had been turtles, or tigers, or even kangaroos.

Ducks?

Really, it seemed impossible. How, and from where?

Ducks, he acknowledged finally. And then, looking closer, and hardly able to believe what he was seeing in detail, Mandarin ducks!

The ducks muttered between themselves: Mandarin ducks, Mandarin ducks … They had heard that expression before, in the pet shop, but had not taken it personally. The dreadful people had simply called them Chinese, whatever that meant. Now the word Mandarin resonated; it felt familiar somehow, welcome ...

The young man with pink hair, wearing ripped jeans and a vintage leather flying jacket, laid his guitar carefully on the back seat, leaned against his rusty jalopy, and had a good think.

He had no idea how the ducks had got there, or who if anyone they belonged to. What was certain was he could not leave them.

Okay, he said, assuming them to understand every word, which of course they could not. But they did feel safer, as if he might have their best interests at heart.

Okay, I'm on my way back down to Wolverhampton. I've been busking since the festival, but now it's way too cold. Playing in the club is okay – but I miss my mum and dad. I want to go home, at least until after Christmas. Then maybe I'll head down to Spain, somewhere warm at least ...

The young musician with pink hair was thinking aloud, pulling on his right pierced ear meditatively, laying out his plans as he went along. The ducks listened appreciatively, but without really understanding a word. He sounded gentle, considerate, helpful ...

There's plenty of water around where I live, the young musician continued. I could drop you off at a canal, for example. My dad's a vet, an animal doctor, so maybe he will know places. Yeah, best you come with me ...

So saying, he disassembled the music magazine stuffed in his back pocket and laid the pages on the back seat, then began to transfer the birds one by one, carefully placing them on a headline here – RODRIGO Y GABRIELA: PLAYING UP A STORM – a photograph there ... He sensed them tensing, even protesting a little at first, but then felt a slow but steady relaxation into softness and acceptance.

He rummaged around for an old metal dish – one used by a dog back home; he would be stopping every few hundred miles for coffee or a toilet, so he could refill it then. Food? That would have to wait. With luck he would make Wolverhampton for breakfast. He just had to get going.

So he did.

The car may have looked like a heap of junk, but it went like the clappers ... when it was going, that is. There were a couple of breakdowns over the next three hundred and fifty or more miles down the M6, including one flat tyre.

But the ducks, accepting collectively that on some profound level they were heading in the right direction, and at a speed that was surprisingly fast, felt reasonably happy (though without knowing why) to go along too.

England

All along the backwater,
Through the rushes tall,
Ducks are a dabbling,
Up tails all.

Kenneth Grahame (Duck's Ditty, The Wind in the Willows)

Somewhere just across the border, on the outskirts of Carlisle, the young musician with pink hair stopped to pick up a boy who said he was on his way to London.

Now I have six hitchhikers, he laughed, glad of the company to help keep him awake.

Six? queried the hitchhiker, who was much younger and (as his driver rightly suspected) had run away from home.

The young musician jabbed his thumb over his shoulder towards the back seat, and the much younger hitchhiker looked, jumped, and yelled DUCKS!

At which, as one, the birds woke, scrambled instinctively to perch as best they could on the guitar case and, in a state of imbalanced disarray, started quack quack quacking like no-one's business ... scared out of their wits.

It took a good long ten minutes for everyone to calm down.

The young musician with pink hair then explained the situation as far as he understood it, which was not much at all. The much younger hitchhiker got over his surprise but wondered if he was allergic to feathers. The ducks hopped back down and lapped up water, noisily as best they could and so managing to get quite a lot over the back seat. Soon the pages of the music magazine were sopping wet as well as despoiled.

But eventually everyone was on the way again, and the birds listened with some contentment to the two young humans voicing to one another.

So, you're off to London then?

Aye, that's the idea.

What will you do there?

Dunno. Get a job, I suppose.

How old are you?

Sixteen.

HOW old?

Fifteen?

The young musician with pink hair dug his passenger in the ribs.

Okay, thirteen, the even younger hitchhiker admitted sheepishly.

Thirteen, thought the young musician. He was twenty-three, a university gradate, and still had no job. As the world became more and more complicated, there were more and more things breaking down. Life was difficult enough, he reckoned. But alone, at thirteen?

He told the much younger hitchhiker about his time in Edinburgh, playing his guitar, singing songs he had written ... fun but not comfortable; interesting but not easy; rewarding, but not financially. He was not much richer now than when he first arrived, he said, which was why he was going home, for a bit at least – assuming the car would hold together.

Home is boring, said the much younger hitchhiker, who was pale and thin and would not last a week in any big city. I hate my parents.

The young musician with pink hair smiled to himself. He remembered saying the same thing when he was that age; it seemed to be an adolescent rite of passage.

So be began to tell stories of his time in Scotland, starting with the one about his first bedsit, with wallpaper so damp it hung off the walls in mouldy folds, and bedbugs, and finishing with a couple about some of the more unconsciously unpleasant people he'd met who tried to make him do things he didn't want to do in exchange for surprisingly large amounts of cash.

He was very good at telling stories. He had such a flair for the dramatic, in fact, that by the time the car drove into Lancaster, the pale thin boy had decided to go back, but to his Aunt Betty's place in Annan: She likes me, he said. And she cooks great sausages.

So the young musician with pink hair let him off at the rail station and gave the much younger hitchhiker a good part of the little money he had saved for a ticket home.

Lounging on the back seat in messy comfort, the ducks were confounded, overwhelmed with information.

Cooks great sausages, had struck a chord with the healthy female.

The leader was more interested in the young musician's tactics to get the even younger human to so successfully turn back.

Home was a word that puzzled them all.

PANDAS?

Another word that had them puzzled was pandas. They heard it for the first time just after Manchester.

The young musician with pink hair was listening to the radio, which they knew was called a radio because he had asked if they would mind him switching it on. I love the radio, he had said, especially at night when driving.

He had been listening to what he said was World Music, but then switched for the news. Did you hear that? he asked, turning his head to make sure the ducks were listening. There are pandas coming to Edinburgh Zoo. Pity we just missed them. They're Chinese too, you know.

Pandas, Chinese pandas they murmered with interest, but only half-awake.

Yeah, they're flying in for Christmas from China, the young musician added.

Flying pandas, thought the ducks sleepily. Interesting.

Nice names too, Tian Tian and Yang Guang, their driver was saying: Sweetie and Sunshine.

Names, they fell asleep, thinking ... why did pandas have names, and not ducks?

WELL DONE, COMPTON

It was near mid-morning by the time the car grumbled its way into the suburbs of Wolverhampton.

Well, thank the gods for that, the young musician with pink hair breathed, stretching out his arms so that that one went across the passenger seat and the other out of his open window.

Well done, Compton, he said next. We made it to Compton. Then laughed and patted the wheel appreciatively.

Compton?

The ducks had been awake for several hours, fretting softly. The backseat was a mess of wetted paper – more papier mache in the making than the dry perches they preferred – and now felt unpleasant and uncomfortable. Also they were starving and wanted to stretch their webbed feet. But Compton sounded an interesting word, so they waited patiently for whatever was to come next.

Darling boy, you're here! What the ...

The warm-sounding woman, who had appeared at the window with different-coloured hair but the same nose, reeled back.

Ducks, she said. And then turned and shouted into the distance, Miles, come and see. Ducks ...

The young musician with pink hair opened his door and slowly unfolded into Compton's suburban sprawl. It was good to be home, he thought. Really good. Then ...

Dad!

So what's this about ducks, said a deeper voice, and a gentle but firm-acting man with the same ears but no piercings peered through a back window.

Mandarin ducks, corrected the young musician.

Chinese Mandarin ducks, confirmed his gentle but firm-acting father. Where on earth did you find them? Not exactly common around these parts. Although, having said that, I did hear that ...

And the voices faded away as the gentle but firm-acting man, the warm-sounding woman and the young musician with pink hair crossed the pavement and disappeared through a gate and up a path into a house.

Now what? grumped the second male duck, who now knew for sure that his elder brother had made the wrong decision.

The healthy female duck clucked disapprovingly. No, they ought to give the humans a chance. Anyway, what were their options?

She was right. In no time at all, the young musician with pink hair and his gentle but firm-acting father were back with a large, well-designed plastic cage, into which they encouraged the five birds to enter one by one.

Ah ha, said the young musician's gentle but firm-acting father. One seems to be hurt. Let's take a look at her inside.

And so the ducks were carried on to the next stage of their journey, leaving behind them a car that would never make a trip like that ever again, and one very soggy and soiled but much appreciated music magazine. Plus a guitar case with even more of a unique provenance than before.

REMARKABLY SECURE

The gentle but firm-sounding man who was an animal doctor lifted each duck onto a table as if handling a precious jewel.

Just look at them, he said to his warm-sounding wife who spent half her time assisting him in the surgery.

Have you ever seen anything so exquisite? Some think the females are nothing compared to the males, but I disagree. The males have the colour, but the females have subtlety.

The ducks, sitting in the pen with clean water and food (that, while not wild, tasted pretty good), preened their feathers.

Well I'm guessing we are the males, said the leader.

And we are the females. But what does subtlety mean?

And the healthy female looked up anxiously as her sister was lifted from her side, out of sight.

The animal doctor man felt around where the damaged wing joined the smaller bird's body.

Mmm, no real damage there.

Then he pulled the wing out to its full extension, but so gently that she did not protest or even murmer. She could sense this human was trying to help, to make her well.

Ahhh, he said, out of joint just here, but not so bad. A few weeks of rest and you'll be just fine. Say in time for the New Year?

And what are you going to do with them until then? his warm-sounding animal assistant wife asked, handing her husband a blanket and calling, Next, please!

Don't they need to get back into water?

The animal doctor man placed the female back in the pen and then covered the cage with the blanket.

Yes. But in the meantime we'll put them in the aviary next door. We don't want them getting upset at cats and dogs and canaries, do we?

And he laughed, but had to straighten his face as first a small girl came into the room carrying her pet rabbit whose normally erect ears had gone floppy. And then a boy with a chameleon that was for some reason no longer changing colour.

The ducks could smell different kinds of smells, hear some very strange noises. But in the darkness they felt warm and, for the first time for a long time, remarkably secure.

FINDING THEIR FEET

Now look, said the young musician with pink hair who was helping his animal doctor father transfer the four healthy birds from the aviary back into the cage several mornings later ... Oi, are you listening?

The ducks had spent an interesting few nights re-learning how to properly perch. It had been a long time since they had been able to sit on branches, as Nature intended, so when they first tried to balance on the rails of the aviary, they kept leaning forwards or backwards, and even falling off.

Now the female with the damaged wing was left alone, which disturbed her greatly because the group had never been separated before. Too traumatised to even perch, she flopped onto the floor of the aviary and dragged into a corner, where she pressed her body against the bars and waited, trembling.

We're going to take you four to water for some exercise, she heard the young musician with pink hair explain next door, but without really understanding. So you have to be good and stay together and come out when told, okay?

The ducks did not need to be told to stay together. On hatching, the first things they had seen were each other; now they were bonded like glue.

They bounced around anxiously as the man and woman the young musician called Mum and Dad carried the cage out into thin pale sunlight and put it in the back of a jeep. Then with the young musician whom Mum and Dad called Jim at the wheel, they drove down the steep hill to Smetstow Brook and found a quiet spot partly under overhanging branches where the water was not completely frozen over.

How old do you think they are? asked Jim as he helped his father place soft nooses of hemp around each of the ducks' necks before encouraging them to the water's edge.

Oh, they're still in their first year. They would have been born last spring. And I'd say they've had little to no experience of living in the wild. More likely they were kidnapped as ducklings and have been in hell every since.

Once called Chinese Teal, they were renamed Mandarins, he added. And first brought to this country – an estate in Sussex – in 1745, possibly by the gardener Capability Brown. I've been reading up on them ...

Trying not to slip on the edge of the brook in his Wellington boots, the animal doctor flicked the ducks' reins as if gee-ing up a herd of horses: Off you go then. Have fun. But not too far ...

Father and son watched the birds paddle and splash, skimming the surface and sometimes dipping their heads underwater in search of food. Occasionally they stretched their wings, but more through instinct than with any clear intention.

Do you think they can fly? asked Jim, hands dug deep into his pockets against the cold. It felt as if the Scottish winter had followed him south; everywhere was frosted, scattered with new snow, the temperature dropping.

Depends how long they were in captivity, and where and how they were kept, replied his father.

Certainly all their wings are weak and need strengthening. I think if we bring them here regularly, they can at least stretch and gain confidence. Then as soon as the snow melts, we can take them up the canal.

Up the canal?

Yes, as I told you when you first arrived, there's a lone Mandarin duck up on a reservoir near Bridgenorth. I read about it in The Guardian last year.

Oh yeah. How did it get there?

No-one knows. It could have escaped from captivity, or maybe it was released deliberately. You know how some people are. They buy animals and then can't be bothered to look after them properly, even if they know how. Drives me crazy. Anyway, come spring, we can take them there.

Would you mind? After all I brought them to you, and I'll be in Spain by then.

No problem. You know what a soft spot I have for Mandarins. It'll be interesting to see what happens, how it all turns out.

SOMETHING NEW AGAIN

It was on the third outing that the second male ventured to dabble a little deeper and rose to the surface with a squark that was more in anger than fear.

It moves! he protested.

What moves? the others asked, gathering around.

The water down below. I could hardly keep my balance to get back up to the surface again. How dare it try to drag me away ...!

Oh my, murmered the leader, and upturned to dabble-dive down to confirm the experience.

Oh yes, he agreed upon a swift return, reminding the others they were surface feeders, not divers.

Something new again, he thought. The only water they had ever known was still and unruffled.

Oh yeah, called Jim, who knew that aquatic birds like Mandarins preferred the calmer waters of ponds and lakes to free-flowing streams and rivers. Be careful of the current. It can be quite strong near the bottom.

Hearing this, the ducks went quiet. There was so much they didn't know about the world, about themselves. If only they could find someone or something like Jim's mother ... someone or something that was a duck teacher and not an occasional veterinary assistant and piano teacher. Someone or something that could give them a quick course in how to be Chinese Mandarin ducks.

The second male was the least interested in the idea, because he was sure he knew enough already. But the leader and his loyal young brother and healthy sister agreed whole-heartedly.

We need a teacher, they affirmed.

Little did they know they were about to find just what they needed.

But not quite yet.

Not until spring.

SPARKLY BOWS

What happened first was that more snow arrived and then Christmas.

The ducks knew something out of the ordinary was happening because the animal doctor's wife – Jim's mum, who was called Laura – tied sparkly bows to their aviary and cage.

And when Jim and his father (whom Laura called Miles) took the quartet to the brook for their regular workout, their halters were made of red ribbon.

By now the brook was iced over completely, and Jim had to smash it along the edges where thinnest to create enough clear water for them to splash around in. He even carried vacuum flasks of hot water to melt thin ice and so ensure they had enough space.

Occasionally passers-by stumbled upon this strange sight and would stop and ask questions but, while polite, Jim and his father gave little away. The last thing the ducks needed were crowds of onlookers and pictures in the local newspaper or on TV.

It was the same back at the house. Much as the motherly female duck was disappointed to have never got as far as the kitchen, they otherwise accepted that the animal doctor respected them for what they were, and had no intention of making them part of the household.

They are wild ducks, he had to say several times to family and friends who wanted to take a look. They were being kept in the aviary out of sight for good reason.

He was right too. The ducks had never been happier. But as they told their sister back in the aviary, they were at their absolute happiest when in the brook, paddling and foraging and feeling out their wings.

She was happiest, she revealed (in a show of strength that surprised them all) when they came back and they were all together again.

They were second happiest when Laura played her piano. The sounds made by young humans who came for lessons were sometimes discordant, but when Laura played, they sank into what might be called a pleasurable state of other-consciousness.

The second male favoured what Jim said was Bach. There was something about the carefully measured sequences of notes that made him feel both alive and harmonious at the same time

The youngest female preferred Brahms. It made her feel soporific ... took her to the edge of sleep but never beyond, and always brought her back again, revived yet at peace.

As for the third male, he liked it when Laura jazzed things up with Jim. Mother and son often played together, even wrote songs together, some sad but others so fast and jolly that he wanted to jump from leg to leg.

But then one day soon after Christmas, Jim was gone.

Off to Spain to help a friend build a house, he had told the ducks, to whom this made no sense at all. Take care, have fun …

Now the sky was grey, the nights long, and when Laura played the piano she sounded bereft. When her pupils played wrong notes, sometimes she snapped at them, even making one young human cry.

In the surgery also, she was not herself. And when she nearly gave a snake the wrong injection, her husband told her to wake up, stop moping and get a grip.

She did eventually. But it took a while. She really missed Jim.

And so – though he tried not to show it – did Jim's dad.

Filling in dark days by helping the ducks get stronger and treating pets with influenza, frozen tails and post-new-year blues, the winter dragged on and on and on ...

DRIP DRIP DRIP

Then one day the ducks noticed a difference.

Jim's father Miles had forgotten to change his boots and not noticed. Laura had forgotten her gloves and not noticed.

The trees all along this particular stretch of the brook were beginning to drip drip drip. And soon the ducks were skating through snow and ice melt as warmer weather began to create ever-widening pools on the surface of the once-wind-chilled frozen water.

A few days later a pale but positive sun put in an appearance, and people began to smile again.

Spring? queried Laura, wrinkling her nose (the one that looked so much like Jim's) and turning her face to the sky.

Spring, confirmed Jim's father, whose ears were so much like his son's, but not pierced.

Which meant everything was about to change completely.

Again.

A SHIFT OF ENERGY

Miles had dreamed of taking the ducks on the family's narrow boat down the canal to Bridgnorth. But moored at Compton Loch, it was still ice-locked and immovable until spring arrived for sure.

We could wait, suggested Jim, who had arrived back unexpectedly from Spain and looked completely different, with sun-bleached hair and skin so brown it was hard to tell where tattoo started and tan ended.

We could wait until it gets even warmer.

No, decided his father. We'll go now, by road.

The ducks were aware that something was happening, a shift of energy in the air. Now healthy and in near-peak condition, they were vibrating with expectation as familiar hands moved them from aviary to cage and so into the jeep.

Still, it came as a surprise when they did not take the usual route to the brook but turned in a quite different direction.

Where are we going?

What's happening?

But no-one felt scared. (Well, the third male did feel slightly more alarmed than usual, but he was not going to admit it to the others.)

They were on the move again.

Ahead, the road stretched into the distance ...

ANOTHER NEW WORD

Ahead, water stretched into the distance ...

The ducks had never seen such a vast expanse of water in their lives before, and they stood along its edge in a state of ecstatic shock, their eyes as wide as ducks' eyes can open.

It's a reservoir, stated Jim, as if this explained everything. It's where we humans reserve and store the water we need to drink to stay alive.

The ducks listened, wondering how much they really understood. Another new word, for sure: reservoir.

And then they saw them ...

Hundreds and hundreds of birds floating on the water.

Family? the ducks murmered amongst themselves.

Best we go and take a look, decided the leader and, jumping in, set off purposefully.

I don't agree, argued the second male, but too late, so he jumped in too.

Ummmm, considered the third male, wanting to follow but not sure. So he jumped in and swam in circles, first one way and then the other to put off the moment of decision.

Come on, let's go, agreed the two females, and gave him the nudge he needed.

Silently Jim and his parents watched them go. There was nothing they could say or do now. They had done the best they could, and now the fate of the ducks lay (as Laura put it) in the lap of the gods.

Good luck, called Jim, who then went home and wrote a cute song with a funky chorus about five Mandarin ducks swimming into the sunset, which much to his surprise became a hit on YouTube and went viral.

AN EXACT REPLICA

The ducks were not having a good time. All their initial excitement dissipated as they met disinterest, dismissal, even hostility, on every side.

Geese in general wanted nothing to do with them.

Swans maintained their dignity until the leading Mandarin had got too close in trying to communicate, then hissed disapproval.

Coots and Terns busied and fussed about and were really not concerned.

As for the Mallards, these wild ducks were downright unfriendly.

And then they saw him.

A male duck – an exact replica of the three male siblings – keeping his distance and swimming alone on the edge of the crowd.

And then HE saw them.

It was a moment none of them would ever forget.

FROM A LONG LINE OF MANDARINS

So don't you know anything? the solitary but accepting male stranger queried, his normally calm demeanour ruffled to have so many demands suddenly laid upon him. He had spent so long alone – moving between Chelmarsh, Anfield and the River Severn to avoid prolonged attention – that reclusivity was almost his second name.

The five newcomers were bobbing about close to shore, not swimming but just maintaining position.

I see I have a lot of work ahead of me, he noted. It's fortunate you found me, because I do know quite a lot about us. But I don't like pressure. So please respect my boundaries and we'll get along just fine.

Yes, he continued, luckily I come from a long line of Chinese Mandarins that feel it imperative to pass on our heritage. Especially since so many of us emigrated or are in exile.

Here already were five words that meant little to nothing to the five new arrivals: Chinese Mandarins, imperative, heritage, emigrated, exile.

We Chinese Mandarins are a bit of an endangered species. (Another expression he had to explain before moving on.)

We number around twenty-thousand pairs worldwide, with a few hanging out in Europe, where we are now, and some to the east, with sightings in Belgium and Hungary, for example, but mostly in Russia, China and Japan. Japan is furthest to the east; go any further and you are on your way back to where you first started. The earth is round, you know.

This all seemed very complicated, if not baffling, but the five kept listening.

Originally Mandarins were high-ranking officials in China – bureaucrats, men who liked organising things and making work for themselves and everyone else, he continued.

Why we're named after them I'm not sure, but maybe they

were rich enough to breed us from other kinds of ducks, or maybe it's because they wore such splendid clothes that other Chinese thought we looked like them.

Where is China? he continued, in response to the question. Far away. Almost as far as Japan, but not quite. It's our home.

The group of five got incredibly excited at this revelation. They had never known where home was. Now they did: China.

Next they learned that the word imperative meant necessary in a bossy kind of way.

Then that heritage referred to the past, especially anything handed down or passed on from long ago.

As to emigrated, this referred to ancestors who had somehow relocated, from China to another part of the world. Why or how, who could tell. Many thousands of tales for sure, some more feathered than others!

For my family's part (the knowledgable male continued) the story is that we were descended from a pair in the Forbidden City in Peking, and that my ancestors were gifted to visitors from London who in turn passed them on to the King and Queen of England. They grew up in Regent's Park Zoo, with ducklings and pairs dispersed all over Britain and beyond.

So you could be a relative, intimated the leading duck of the five.

I could indeed. Now tell me about yourselves …

You forgot about explaining exile, corrected the second male duck, pleased to note that this know-it-all was not wholly perfect.

Ah, exile. Well, I'm sorry to say we are all exiles. Not personally banished from our home country but forced by circumstance of heritage to live a long time abroad.

But now we are free, noted the younger female, flexing her wings and pleased to feel them so in balance. We could fly home.

The others looked askance at her presumption and foolishness.

Whereupon she backed down with a Sorry, silly, forget what I said.

And so – superficially at least – peace was restored. Superficially because, in the mind of the older bird, the seed of an idea had been planted.

As for the five siblings, they were united in a different kind of excitement. They had found their teacher.

MY NAME IS CHUNG

Every day, towards the end of the afternoon, as the sun grew more confident amid the rain and showers of early spring, the ducks would meet for their daily lesson.

The older bird would look at them sagely over his beak and ask, So what do you want to learn today?

We would like to know about names, the leader had said, soon after first arriving. We have noticed that humans use a similar sound when calling or talking to one another and we think these sounds are called names.

That's right, said the teacher. So what do you want to know?

Well, do we have names?

You mean you don't?

Recalling that the flying pandas from China had names, but they did not, the five looked from one to another and then ruffled their feathers to the negative.

Good heavens, said the teacher. But what did your parents call you?

We can't remember, said the older female sadly. We can't even remember their faces, where we came from.

The teacher whistled even more sagely under his duck breath.

Now I understand why you keep calling me teacher. My name is Chung, which means wise one. My father named me so when I was first hatched. Apparently I emerged from my shell knowing everything there was to know. Since then (and here he laughed in a wise Mandarin duck-like way) I have been slowly forgetting, devolving rather than evolving. Meeting you is good for my memory, so ask away ...

Chung, they all repeated, getting their vocal cords and beaks around the sound. Chung.

Chung looked the oldest male sibling straight in the eye and named him Shing.

Shing means victory, he explained, and it is a victory that you have led your brothers and sisters this far.

Remembering the brother and sister who were taken away one day by the dreadful man into the shiny kitchen and never seen again, the leading duck was not sure he deserved such an accolade, and said so.

Such honesty and compassion makes you great rather than victorious, said Chung, reconsidering. So I re-name you Cong.

And you, he said, turning to the second oldest male who was prickling with self-righteousness, are forthwith called Dewei, meaning of great principle.

Dewei preened with the pleasure of knowing that his strict moral code was so clear for all to see.

Naming the youngest male was trickier because sometimes his reactions were quite erratic, contradictory even. Having made note of this, Chung thought long and hard.

Hmmm. I have been veering between Ho for goodness, and Jun for truth. But now I am leaning towards Shuang, for bright, clear and open-hearted. For some reason, I think it might be more helpful. (Give you something to work towards and keep you focussed, he was thinking.)

The third male mulled over the sounds and meanings: Ho, Jun and Shuang; goodness ... truth ... or bright, clear and open-hearted.

I like Ho, said Cong.

I prefer Jun, said Dewei.

Then I will be Shuang, he decided, and in so choosing defied his elder brothers, pleased Chung, and above all else remained true to himself.

Cong, Dewei and Shuang immediately seemed larger and more confident. They had names; they knew who they were.

When it came to the females, it was simpler because their characters were even more clearly defined.

How about Hu-tu, after the goddess of the earth? Chung suggested for the older female.

Excellent, the others agreed. She looks after us all, mothers us … she's always on hand to help.

Hu-tu preened with a pleasure more than a little tinged with vanity. She was a goddess.

When it came to naming the younger female – the quiet placatory baby of the family and now quite lovely following recuperation and rehabilitation – it was even easier: Bo, for precious.

They were all so excited and happy they swam in a circle for over an hour, chanting their names: great Cong … principled Dewei … bright, clear and open-hearted Shuang … earth goddess Hu-tu … and precious Bo.

Wise Chung paddled on the sidelines, grunting with contentment.

It had been a good session, a very good day's work.

SO MANY QUESTIONS

And so the days passed into weeks and even months. All the snow and ice finally melted away to raise the level of the water even higher, and the weather grew balmy. Soon the reservoir was fringed with green, and there were flowers ...

The ducks learned about trees and grass and flowers one week, then animals, insects and reptiles through another. While in between, Chung explained the sky above, with its sun, moon and stars, the earth below, and how water and air were the keys to life.

Birds, of course, took rather longer as the information was so much more personal. Also, there was so much to know. They learned, for example, that they belonged to a tribe called Anatidae, order Anseriformes, class Aves, and with the scientific name *Aix galericulata*. That these terms were in an ancient human language called Latin; that academically the names of ducks were capitalised, but in fiction it was okay not to worry too much.

Is it important to remember all these names? asked Bo, whose head was hurting so much she was ready to switch off.

Definitely, decreed Dewei, who took extensive notes in his head.

Remember what is important and interesting to you, suggested Chung. It's not possible to remember everything as you grow older. I have forgotten many things I learned and used to know. But I retain what I suppose I choose on some level to retain.

Dewei went quiet at this revelation. But not for long, because he had so many questions of his own ... And many came from genuine curiosity and not simply reaction for reaction's sake.

For one thing, he wanted to know how he had come into being, to which the others woo-wooed in agreement. They too were experiencing unusual feelings that they didn't know quite how to handle.

ESPECIALLY BEAUTIFUL

Chung dipped his head underwater to recover his equilibrum; it was not a topic he had really voiced before. Then he raised his crest to the sky. Finally he looked the mini-flock of five (as straight as he was able) in their ten eyes, and did his best.

You are males, called drakes, he told Cong, Dewei and Shuang. In general you protect and organise.

And you are hens, he assured Hu-tu and Bo, but not hens as in chickens. You lay eggs from which ducklings emerge, just as you all did some time a year ago. This is how we keep our tribe – our family – alive.

To prove his point, he told them all to look around, to where pairs of geese and swans, coots and terns and mallards were making nests and laying eggs. Already new-born hatchlings were beginning to clutter the water with noise and excitement, and adult birds displaying far more aggression than usual.

In spring, Cong explained, your bodies awaken after the long winter sleep and you feel so alive with excitement you want to reproduce and have your own families. So each male sets out to woo a female as his partner ...

Every female is seen as extremely precious, he continued (at which Bo preened with pleasure). So males have to work hard to attract the opposite sex. (And here he nodded again to Cong, Dewei and Shuang.) Your plumage gives you a head start, of course; that's why you have been created so especially beautiful.

And he remembered how hard he had had to work to persuade his own partner to join him, and then the ducklings they had raised before she died.

We do not live so long, he told the group. This is my sixth season, so I am nearing the end of my life. But this is a matter of no concern to me; I am just waiting to be reunited with my partner.

He also remembered, a day soon after he had arrived (a sole exotic immigrant, causing much interest among the townspeople of Bridgnorth), a woman standing on the water's edge talking with a man with a camera and microphone, saying, "These Chinese Mandarins are like little paintings. Their plumage is just so beautiful."

Cong, Dewei, Shuang, Hu-tu and Bo looked at one another? Were they beautiful, they wondered?

In answer to which Chung led them to an area of flat water,

where sunlight sparkled on blue reflected from the sky above, and told them to look down and study themselves with care in the mirror-like surface.

And they looked. And for the first time, in recognising their exceptional beauty, accepted that they were very special indeed.

TESTING THEIR WINGS

How are you at flying these days? Chung asked the group one fine morning.

He had been watching them try their wings out, day after day.

How far do you think you can go?

Cong took off and skimmed the surface to the far side of the reservoir.

Dewei flew higher to circle the water, so avoiding other birds taking off and landing.

Shuang and Hu-tu flew together, to where a group of young humans – children – were standing on the edge of the water, watching, pointing and throwing bread.

Bo flew prettily, first one way and then the other and then flopped back down.

Chung chided her, told her to get off her backside and do better, so grumbling slightly she took off again and joined Shuang and Hu-tu in being admired.

How do you feel about making a trip? Chung said later, as they fed together.

The others looked up, interested.

Where to? they asked.

China, he replied, back-paddling fast to avoid what he thought might be a furious reaction. Instead there was a long silence while the five younger ducks took this in.

Cong had no doubts. They could do it.

Dewei listed the pros and cons and considered …

Shuang felt equal amounts of terror, curiosity and excitement.

With mating in mind, Hu-tu imagined all the other male ducks they might meet.

And Bo, who would have been quite happy not to fly another inch, decided to go along with whatever the others decided.

When to do we start? asked Cong, speaking for them all.

Tomorrow, replied Chung. We must take advantage of the weather and fly as far as we can as quickly as we can.

Will it take long? asked Bo, plaintively.

Dewei flapped her affectionately with his wing. Of course, you ninny, he admonished. It's halfway around the world, remember.

Which way do we go? Do we have a map? asked Cong.

The map is inside me. I follow my instinct, my feelings. We will head for Belgium.

Belgium, they fluttered, ready for anything.

But first we need to make a call. Fly northeast across country to drop in at York.

The five put their collective heads to one side as if to ask why.

It is a place of great interest, replied Chung, shedding a small cloud of white duck down into the fresh but muddied water to emphasise the point. But he refused to be drawn any further.

NO TIME FOR SIGHTSEEING

The ancient city of York lay some one hundred miles across country, as the duck flies. Which is a very long way if you have never flown far before. But all that winter exercise proved invaluable, and they were surprised to discover that by pacing themselves, and breaking the trip into short, sharp bursts of activity, with rest periods in between, they were able to cover the ground in no time at all.

Travelling down from Scotland to Compton, huddled in dazed fashion on the back seat of the car, or slipping and sliding off Jim's guitar case, they had seen nothing. Now the island part of the earth known as England lay below them, stretching in all directions, and full of distractions. But what lay ahead drew them onwards; as a destination Belgium left no time for idle sightseeing.

This was not say that Chung allowed them to pass the time without pointing out this and that, as he felt that the details of villages, towns, rivers and lakes and mountain ranges would add to the knowledge they were rapidly recollecting and accumulating.

Since it was hard to communicate on the wing, he would take advantage of each rest stop to tell them what to look for on the next leg.

I had been planning to fly around the outskirts of Crewe, he mused, as they first rested on the River Trent west of Shrewsbury; I think you must have passed through it on your way down from Scotland. Now we'll head up between Manchester and Sheffield. In that way we will avoid Manchester Airport. We don't want to get tangled up with any kind of aircraft: dangerous for everyone.

And he explained how birds on the wing sometimes got sucked into engines and caused accidents.

Everyone shivered at the thought of what would happen to both them, and all the humans who might lose their lives too. Humans could be just as thoughtlessly cruel, standoffish, unfriendly and uncooperative as geese, swans, coots and terns and mallards. But, equally, humans could be kind and helpful too. The five knew this now.

They flew in a line, with Chung leading the way, and Hu-tu in the rear, keeping an eye on Bo and making sure she did not fall behind.

Cong paid careful attention to the flight path, for Chung had already told him that at some point soon, he would have to take over.

Dewei grumbled disagreeably. Shuang tried to jolly everyone up.

Look, he called as they flew through a small cloud: Now you see me, now you don't.

To which they all laughed, in a duck-like way. Yes, even Dewei, who knew in his heart he was being a critical pain in the neck and for the first time ever wished he could stop.

Such a wish proved to be a life-changing experience. By the time they reached York, having become so aware of how awful he sounded every time he opened his beak to moan, he had taken the first important step towards being a very different duck indeed.

A SURPRISED RUFFLE OF FEATHERS

Excuse me, Teacher Chung, he said so politely as they glided down onto the River Ouse that, without exception, all his siblings raised their eyebrows. Or rather they would have lifted eyebrows if they had been graced with such things. Instead it was more a surprised ruffle of head feathers ...

I was just wondering, what we are doing here? Why have we flown back up north when we need to go east? Belgium is that way, he said pointedly. Not this way.

Chung reflected upon the question. It was, after all, perfectly valid.

We are here to find my son, he said quietly. And he told them how he had raised several broods of ducklings on Cannop Ponds in the Forest of Dean, where he and his mate had made their home, along with others of their own species.

We lost many, of course ... To foxes, rats, snakes, human intervention. But quite a few survived and continue to live and breed there – the most successful colony of Mandarins in the whole of this country. But after my partner died, I could not bear to stay, so I flew just a short distance north and took up residence in the area where you found me.

But why do you think your son might be here? interrupted Cong.

Lok? He was always curious about the world, wanting to see and do everything. Upset after his mother died, we argued one day about some trivial matter and the next day he just took off ... I heard on the grapevine that he was in or near York.

What's a grapevine? asked Bo innocently, never having seen or heard of such a thing before.

In this sense it means an unofficial means of carrying out communication ... by quack of beak, so to speak. Back on Chelmarsh Reservoir I heard from a touring Canadian goose that a fat Mandarin had been observed making its way down the Ouse, and I thought, that's my boy.

Um, why would your son be fat? asked Dewei, unsurely, not wanting to cause offence.

Eats, eats, eats ... never stops. His mother said she had never known such an appetite, that she'd had to work so hard to keep him fed that she'd lost half her own duck weight.

Excuse me, he called to a passing female Bufflehead sitting on her nest in the trunk of an old poplar hanging over the water. Have you seen a fatter version of myself on the river anywhere?

The rare North American Bufflehead – escaped from a zoo and taking time out to raise a brood on her own way home, but heading west – hissed gently, warning them to keep their distance. Her Canadian partner would be back soon. Maybe he would know.

And he did.

THATTAWAY!

The group of six spent the entire day searching the stretch of water where the male Bufflehead said he had last seen Chung's son.

That night Chung perched alone.

The next morning they set off paddling down towards York and began asking other water birds they met along the way about sightings.

A heron proved to be so focussed on standing on one leg that there was no response at all.

Moorhens were too busy darting this way and that to spare a second.

However, a pair of Mute swans thought, maybe.

A gander of geese reckoned, possibly.

And a family of wild ducks said they seemed to remember ... but then proved to have forgotten whatever it was they remembered, if anything.

Chung swam slowly. He felt dispirited, which worried the others because, despite all the things they had learned, without him they would surely be lost again.

But then they passed a small rowboat gently bobbing up and down on the chop other river traffic was creating, and an elderly, silver-haired man meditatively holding a stick and line into the water looked up as they passed and exclaimed in surprise, Oh, more of you?

The ducks stopped in mid-stroke, and back-paddled furiously against the current.

No, no, keep going, the elderly, silver-haired man said and – quite forgetting that he was fishing – pointed his rod downriver. They went thattaway: one like you two (pointing at Hu-tu and Bo) and one like the rest of you, only fatter.

Chung flapped his wings, becoming so excited he ruffled up his feathers to twice his normal size.

Yes, as fat at that, laughed the elderly, silver-haired man, and went back to a quiet contemplation of his life, past, present and future, though mostly simply enjoying the beauty of the morning and musing on how great at his age it felt to be alive.

PADDLING THROUGH THE CITY CENTRE

Chung felt invigorated also. Hopeful again, he took off to fly the last stretch into York itself. But first he took the group on a detour to follow its ancient wall and defensive barbicans. He then led them back to the water's course, sometimes diving under and over bridges but otherwise skimming the surface so as to keep a close eye on other water birds in the vicinity.

He was so enthused by the beauty and historic riches of the ancient city that he began teaching again, on the wing.

York had been inhabited by humans for at least eight thousand years, he advised. In the old days she was a major port; vessels would come up the Humber from the estuary and tie up to unload and load goods. But then climate change caused the river to silt up, and trading came to a halt. That's when Hull became prosperous … until humans fished out the North Sea.

We'll be flying past later, when we've found Lok, he concluded.

Ah-hum, coughed Cong gently. But the man in the boat said They, not He. I think that means your son may not be alone.

Chung ah-hummed in reply. He was not deaf, he snapped in a very unwise Chung fashion. He had heard the word They too. Well, whoever Lok had in tow, he would be happy for the hen to tag along. Right now, though, he could only think about finding his son again, fat or not.

It was interesting passing through the city. By staying in the centre of the river, and navigating any passing traffic, they managed to avoid too much attention. But they did catch the eyes of those on pleasure boats and cruisers. Or rather they caught the eyes (mostly) of children, and the younger they were, the more excited and curious they became.

There were also, of course, the birdwatchers.

Caught in the wake of one boat, they heard an especially interesting exchange between a boy with red hair and the sandy-grey-haired birdwatcher they supposed must be his father. In one hand, the older human was handling a pair of what the ducks now knew, from their experience on the reservoir, to be binoculars. In the other, he held what looked like a thin book but Chung recognized as an iPad.

See, the man was saying authoritively, reading and chatting at the same time: See the male? Looks a bit like the Red-Crested Pochard, but the colouring's different. See the red bill, the reddish face with large white crescents over the eyes, and what look like whiskers? See now, as that one rears up and flaps its wings, you can see the breast is purple, with two vertical white bands, reddish flanks and those two striking two areas of orange on its back that resemble sails.

Yes, dad. I can see ... the boy with red hair was saying, a small hardback digest about waterbirds in his own hands. Then under his breath: I am eight, you know. I can read too.

But his father was too absorbed to catch the hurt tone in his son's voice. He had moved on to the female of the species, describing her (without even lifting his eyes from the screen) as being similar in shape, but with a white eye-ring and a stripe that runs back from the eye, plus a small white stripe on the flank and the tip of her bill pale compared to that of the male.

Thus described, the ducks and humans passed by one another in a state that can only be described as mutual observation.

Ships that pass in the night, observed Chung.

The others looked expectant, awaiting illumination.

Chung explained how we all have our path in life, always moving forward, but are intermittently joined by others, who stay and then leave again of their own volition in their own time.

Like the smaller rivers joining the Ouse ... observed Bo, cleverly connecting the dots.

Or the driver of the box on wheels, the van, who helped us along without even knowing we were there ... (Dewei)

Or the young musician Jim, who gave us our best lift ... (Hu-tu)

Or his kind mother and father who nursed us back to health and set us free ... (Shuang)

Or Chung, who is here to stay ... said Cong, with deep-felt relief.

As long as I am able, Chung added pragmatically, looking from one to the other in a kindly fashion. It was important, though, he said, to also not forget those who seem not to help at all ... quite the contrary, in fact, because in a way they are the most important teachers of all.

Remembering how their lives had been stolen away, how they had been treated first in the pet shop, and then by the ignorant people who dumped them without a second thought, Cong saw red. One hundred per cent sure he had learned nothing from that period of his life but hate, he discounted them completely.

Luckily a passing canoe provided a distraction, and the powerful wave of emotion fell away almost as swiftly as it had arisen.

Let's go, he suggested, steadfastly putting any remaining resentment on a back burner. Let's fly.

So they did, but not far, because almost as soon as they had taken to the air, a large natural space presented itself on the west bank, with woodlands and walks, drifts of spring flowers and plenty of simply splendid perches for spending the night: Rowntree Park.

ATTACK!

It was very dark among the trees along the riverbank. The moon was hidden behind thick clouds, and despite knowing there was nothing he could do, Chung felt enormous frustration. Where was Lok? Where could he be?

Chung knew he couldn't keep the younger ones hanging around for much longer. They had already flown many more miles than they needed to, and had done so just to please him. Now time was running out. They had to move on.

It was late when they decided to head for the park's large pool for a late feed. They sensed many nesting birds congregated on its numerous small islands, built especially to keep them safe.

Or were they?

As the six Mandarins foraged around the edge, skimming the surface of the water, Cong suddenly became aware of two large human shapes emerging from a trail, one with a torch and the other with a net and a large bag. They were creeping as quietly as they could (which was not quietly at all by non-human standards).

Cong nudged Dewei, who passed the message along to the others.

They all knew, either instinctively or from some deep-seated indelible memory, what the two humans were up to. As the men waded into the water, the Mandarins began to send out warning signals that quickly woke the sleeping birds on or around the pond, and had them flapping and screaming in panic, trying desperately to distract the thieves away from their nests.

Come on, said Cong without a second of hesitation. Attack!

And he flew at the men, swiftly followed by Dewei and Shuang, and even Bo, who showed a surprising degree of aggressive energy for a bird normally so passive and sweet.

Chung, who was suddenly feeling his age, waited with Hu-tu, who was tut-tutting that she hoped they would not get hurt, and how best to help?

Confused by the sudden beating of wings about their heads, one thief dropped his torch, which only made things worse: neither of the men could see a thing. Then one stumbled as Cong clipped his ear, falling face forwards into the water.

By now the pond was pandemonium.

Panic-stricken parents (mostly ducks of one kind or another) and their offspring rushing to and fro, turning the dark water white with froth.

Two adult humans effing and blinding, struggling to get their bearings and wanting only to escape.

The Mandarins, aquiver with a fear that was transforming into a sense of victory: to have saved any number of ducklings from the fate that had once so nearly been their own end.

Wow, wheezed Cong, who had used up all his voice in waking up the entire park.

Hurray! hooted Bo, who had surprised herself in taking such bold action.

Unbelievable, ululated Shuang, who felt great to have taken sides and come up trumps.

I have to say, I'm surprised at myself, snorted Dewei, who normally steered clear of trouble in order to protect his image.

Well done, congratulated Chung, who could see the lights of a vehicle approaching. Let's leave the park rangers to sort out the mess. I think we all need a good rest after all that.

It was certainly a relief to return to their perches and get a bit of sleep.

But this surprising night was not over yet.

When they woke at dawn, they were no longer six. They were eight.

THE SQUABBLING COUPLE

We saw you, watched you, explained Lok. But it was so dark that at the time we were not sure what you were or who you were. Also I'd had a huge supper and could hardly move. But after things quietened down, the rain stopped, the clouds cleared and we saw you up here.

He was indeed a very fat duck compared to the rest of them. He made his father look quite small, especially when they sat side by side.

Excuse me, but what about me? demanded Lok's mate, signalling extreme disapproval to her partner. Isn't it time you introduced me properly?

She was in her third spring, she explained confidently with hugely dramatic gestures, with the name Li Qin, which meant a beautiful stringed musical instrument: beautiful to look at, beautiful to play, beautiful to listen to.

The five siblings moved closer together on the branch. Even Chung looked slightly intimidated by his new daughter-in-law, whom Lok had partnered the previous year.

Yes, this third female was very different to the others. For one thing she was older. For another she was not warm and motherly. Nor was she a gentle peacemaker.

The sisters viewed her warily. Was this noisy, theatrical Mandarin going to upset the balance of the group? Because it was clear that she and Lok – whose name meant happy – had arrived to stay.

It was when Chung had explained the trip, assuming his son and partner would be coming along, that things got tricky. Lok was amenable to the idea, but reluctant to leave the river that provided such rich pickings.

We like it here, he explained simply. Humans just love me; some even bake cakes and bring them along ... I'm very partial to chocolate!

No wonder you're so fat, commented his father, dryly.

It's true, you are fat, agreed Li Qin fondly. But I remember you being quite trim when we first got together. Maybe some travelling would be good for you, slim you down. You're always talking about going here and there, doing this and that ...

And you? What about you? Lok came back in a flash. You like your home comforts too, I seem to remember. But at the same time you're always angsting about your age, and how all your talents are going down the drain.

Talents? Everyone but happy-go-lucky Lok was deeply curious.

Well, let me see, Li Qin began, counting on her webbed toes. I can play, I can sing, I can organise ...

Cong and Dewei felt a frisson of anxiety. Organising was their bag.

I'm good with other ducks and humans too ...

Hu-tu hissed under her breath. Caring for others was her vocation.

I love debating, a good argument ...

Bo tucked her beak into her chest feathers. Normally she hated any kind of confrontation.

At the same time my dear partner could sell the tail feathers off a peacock, added Lok, proudly.

And obviously is never lost for words, noted Chung, even more wryly. Still, we are in need of a good diplomat on this trip, one that knows the ways of the Mandarin. And a duck that can keep us upbeat and entertained at the best and worst of times is surely an asset.

He told the group simply and clearly that they would all have an equal part to play in the journey ahead. One duck was no more important than any other, even Lok, his own offspring. They were a team.

But Lok and Li Qin were not listening. While affectionately preening one another, they were bickering away again, this time about where to go for breakfast and how wonderful it was for Lok to have found his father – or his father find him; there was also the condition of Li Qin's plumage, which in her eyes (but no others), surely seemed a little tired and listless.

Finally Chung lost patience – while thrilled to find Lok again, he was also remembering why their relationship had been fraught in the first place! – and decided to blow caution to the wind.

I'm off, he announced, as flickers of morning sunlight began to filter through the whispering leaves of the riverbank willows. Are you coming?

A BEAKFUL OF SALT WATER

They fell into a ragged line, with only Lok and Li Qin arguing about who should be ahead of whom.

Down the flowing Ouse they flew, until Lok begged for a rest, and Li Qin begged – winningly – for everyone's indulgence.

You can see how out of shape he is, she entreated. Just give him a bit of leeway and he'll soon be as fit as the rest of you.

So they landed near the village of Foxfleet, where Lok immediately plunged into the river in chase of an especially luscious-looking small fish.

Yuuuuuuk, he screeched, returning to the surface with no more than a beakful of salt water. It tastes disgusting!

Now now, his father soothed. You gave me no time to explain; this is where salty tidal water from the Humber estuary joins the fresh water of the river. I'm afraid it's salt water from here on, right across to the other side.

The other side of what? asked Lok.

The North Sea, replied Chung.

Sounds exciting, his son replied, the unexpected taste in his mouth suddenly quite forgotten. Let's go ...

FACING THE CHALLENGE

There was just one more stop before commencing the flight over the sea.

Chung thought they all needed to think seriously about what they were doing, the long journey they were embarking upon. Because it was more than likely that they would never come back.

Whatever your feelings about and your experiences of Scotland and England, this island has been your home. It's where you were born. I want to make sure you are all one hundred per cent sure.

Sitting on the tidal flats off Grimsby, the sky clear but the coastal winds cold and bracing, Cong, Dewei, Shuang, Hu-tu and Bo huddled together and quickly agreed that, while afraid, they also felt they had no choice. Only one thing was sure: as long as they stayed together, everything would work out just fine.

They then had to sit for what seemed like an eternity, or at least until the tide began to turn, while Lok and Li Qin disputed over whether to stay or whether to go.

Such arguing frightened Bo. She was sure they would kill one another at any moment; it all sounded so serious.

Hu-tu felt more anxious than alarmed. Perhaps they would agree to get counselling; they certainly needed some form of help.

The three brothers were less generous. Cong suggested a short sharp slap; Dewei thought them totally selfish and egotistical;

and Shuang shape-shifted from one point of view to another, while feeling extremely annoyed to be wasting so much time.

In the end, of course, all the bickering was nothing but hot air. Lok was all in favour of a huge adventure, or any number of smaller adventures wrapped into one; Li Qin admitted to being wholly driven by ambition, and the thousand and one chances that surely lay ahead.

With sighs of relief all round, they were able to stand in a line and, facing north, bow low: with gratitude for a great escape.

They then turned to face the way they had come, from the west, and bowed low: with gratitude for all that had been.

They turned again, this time to the south, and bowed once more: with gratitude for what might have been.

Finally they turned their beaks east, and bowed especially low: with gratitude for whatever was to come.

They then formed a tight circle, touched wings and after a few minutes of silence, with the tide running fast and already wetting their webbed feet, Cong took off and led the way. Chung watched and nodded, taking his place in the rear so that now he could keep an eye on stragglers.

Their challenging leader was in the challenging lead again.

The North Sea

The son of a duck is a floater. (Like father, like son...)

Arab Proverb

The land quickly fell behind and Lok was soon in trouble. While he was brave, his body weight was a hindrance, yet he knew he had no one to blame but himself, his own epicurean habits.

I eat too much. I talk too much, he admitted inwardly. I dissipate my energy and my talents right, left and centre. I am my own worst enemy. But there again, if we don't rest soon, I'm going to have a heart attack.

Luckily there were any number of seagoing vessels plying carefully plotted routes below them, and when he veered off to commence an unexpected but apparently desperate downward glide path, the others swiftly followed.

What are we doing here? asked Bo, settling against the side of a container that offered a great view of the sea below and all around, and fluffing out her plumage to stay warm. It's freezing.

Hu-tu huddled close to share her own body heat, explaining that Lok needed to get his breath.

None of them could believe their eyes; it was a landscape – seascape – like no other. All around, the floundering steely waters moved gleaming and alive, scattered about with boxes of every size, some stacked with more boxes and seeming to touch the sky.

Chung was shouting against the wind to anyone who cared to listen, that way below the sea was anywhere up to seven hundred metres deep ... well over a third of the length of the wall around York, he quickly worked out. Imagine!

Dewei was trying to imagine; he was also looking down the wall of the constantly shifting pile of containers on which they were resting and trying not to feel so dizzy. That deep?

When he told Hu-tu that he had vertigo, she fluffed and puffed with laughter. Normally she might have commiserated, but this was ridiculous.

How can you have vertigo? she cackled, Mandarin-style. You're a duck.

But looking up and down and all around, everything appeared so alien; even Chung had to admit to never having seen metal walls before. Especially metal walls of so many different colours and stamped with such an assortment of symbols.

Why are humans always building walls? shouted Bo against the wind, as a way to forget how cold she was feeling. We crossed one coming down south from Scotland, built from coast to coast by someone called Hadrian. I remember thinking when Jim told us, how strange ...

There was a long silence while they all thought about walls, and also barriers and boundaries.

Chung waited, hoping that at long last they were remembering how to think for themselves. And was delighted when it was Lok – Lok, his runaway, happy-happy-happy-go-lucky, fun-seeking son – who replied ... and with a remarkable display of innate wisdom, all things considered:

Humans build walls to protect themselves and their interests against those they fear might try to take them away and expose additional weaknesses.

Humans create barriers to keep themselves apart from those who have different ideas, fearfully avoiding conflict, challenge and change.

Humans create boundaries to keep others at a distance, as self-protection.

Chung reflected on how true this was of his own situation: the wall he had raised after the death of Lok's mother; the barriers created to separate himself from the past; and the boundaries he had set to avoid genuine intimacy.

This was a marvellous piece of self-realisation for a duck of infinite wisdom (though, as he acknowledged internally, little apparent common sense). As Chung took off again to follow the others, he saw Cong release a small blue feather that floated down into the ocean to became one with the sea water that spread all around the world.

ALTERED STATES

As they flew on, the eight ducks began to relax into what could only be described as an altered state of consciousness.

First the beat of their wings found a certain synchronicity and then, without any signal or predetermined thought, with the port and cityscape of Rotterdam looming on the far horizon, they moved into a staggered and reasonably balanced V-formation, with Cong in the lead, then Dewei and Shuang, Lok and Li Qin, Hu-tu and Bo, and Chung.

There had been no need to make adjustments; each duck had found its natural position in the flight pattern. As they flapped their wings, disturbing the air and leaving swirling eddies behind them, they were all, except for Cong of course, able to save energy by finding support in the wake of the bird in front.

When Cong grew tired, the next in line – Dewei, as it happened – automatically moved up to take the lead, and so they flew on, each taking their turn, each taking responsibility.

It was not perfect – they could all feel an imbalance – but it was far more comfortable than before.

Dewei allowed himself a mental detour to the north, to check out the oil and gas rigs that dotted the North Sea. Chung had cleverly managed to avoid them, but Dewei was curious to know more about why humans were exploiting and hurting the earth they shared with all other living things. It seemed against the laws of nature. It seemed unjust.

Shuang shifted between resisting authority and needing to feel safe. It made his stomach churn; it made him feel anxious. Sometimes he could not understand himself at all. If he respected Chung so much, why did he also resent the depth of his knowledge and wisdom? If he admired Cong for being so fearless and sure, why did he envy his leadership qualities?

Hu-tu was dreaming of solving all the problems of her little family. She imagined herself as heroically indispensable, endlessly giving and being rewarded in equal measures. Did worrying about the others stop her worrying about herself? she wondered, with a fleeting moment of perception.

Bo was not enjoying herself but kept quiet, wanting only the best for everyone else. Sometimes she was the only one all the others were talking to, because she refused to take sides. But it meant her own feelings remained locked up. Like whatever was locked up in all those metal boxes, those containers.

Lok was running through what he knew about Belgium, because like his father, he was a great source of knowledge, even if much of it was food and pleasure-related. Blue mussels, he was dreaming. He would need rocky outcrops and beaches for those. And chocolate, Belgian chocolate. How could he locate plentiful supplies of that?

Li Qin was quickly recognising that Rotterdam could be a splendid place to launch her career as … as what? No matter. Just present her with an opportunity – any opportunity – and this sharp cookie would shine; she'd be ready to give it her all, one hundred per cent. There was just one problem …

Lok, she called, returning from her own inner dreamscape and seeing the industrious spread of the enormous port – third largest in Europe – lying ahead.

Can you catch up with whoever is in the lead and tell them we're off course? This is not Belgium. This is Holland.

The Netherlands-Belgian Border

It's as hard to see a woman crying as it is to see a barefooted duck.

Irish proverb

Cong was terribly embarrassed. They were bobbing about in a dock, taking stock.

We can't stay here, Li Qin stated decisively. It's getting dark. And this water smells disgusting, of oil and who knows what else. Can't we just get out of the city and make a plan in the morning?

Chung agreed; his son's mate was not just a pretty face. He was tired too.

Fly inland, he ordered. I believe the countryside is quite lovely once you get out of Rotterdam. It's the Gateway into Europe, you know. Follow the River Meuse ... fly under or over the Erasmus Bridge, keep going ...

So they lifted off, relieved to leave such crude-slicked waters, milling with so much flotsam and jetsam, including rotting sea food so stinking that even Lok turned up his beak. How could humans be so careless with their most valuable commodities? Water, marine life, food ...

Saddened, perplexed and, above all, exhausted, they followed the shining ribbon of river until lights fell away and the darkness of night prevailed.

Cong peered ahead for a suitable landing place and alighted only when a secure-looking-feeling perch offered itself on the side of a building. Almost flying into it, almost on top of it, he saw something sticking out, grabbed and held on. They were higher than he would have liked, but after that sky-scraping container vessel, the smell of soil-rich earth was comfortingly close

Goodnight, said Cong. Sorry.

But the others were already sound asleep.

ON THE MOVE

They were woken by a big noise, a shifting of gears, and the shocking sensation of suddenly being on the move.

Eeee, screeched Hu-tu. I'm falling ...

Geee, gasped Bo. I'm sinking ...

Arahhh, yelled Lok. I'm bottoming out ...

Whaaa, cried Li Qin. I'm moving sideways ...

Whooo, wailed Shuang. I'm going up ...

Wowww, whooped Cong, Dewei and Chung in unison. We're going up ... and round ... and down again ...

It's a windmill, said an unfamiliar voice. You're perched on a windmill and now it's started work again.

They looked around and saw that they were standing on four enormous sails or vanes, all turning in unison and attached to a tall building made of wood.

I'm up here, said the voice again. On top of the mill. Milling, grinding ...

The eight ducks going round and round felt not only giddy but completely at a loss.

Where are you? called Chung. We can't see you and have no idea what you're saying. What language are you speaking?

The voice laughed, then tossed down just one word: Mandarin.

CHII-NII'S MILL

It was lucky this new duck was familiar with all the languages of the world, which she said came to her as naturally as breathing. Not only did she know English, but also Dutch and Flemish. Best of all, though, for the others to hear China's predominant language spoken like a native was indeed a gift from heaven.

I am Chii-nii, goddess of spinners, weavers and dreams, she said by way of introduction. I have been waiting for you.

Waiting for us? How did you know we were coming?

Oh, so much is on its way back to China, she replied. The pandas of course have been taken in the wrong direction, but everything else ... eastwards.

Like what? What else is going back to China?

Things. Humans, people. And now it would seem also, its indigenous birds.

What kind of things? What human beings, what people?

The group of eight was all agog. But before going any further circling round and round, which seemed not to be getting them anywhere but feeling airsick, they thought they should get off, recover their equilibrum and take stock.

Whilst not knowing anything in detail about things and people and other birds returning to China, Chung was relieved to say that at that precise moment, he knew exactly where they were.

Kinderdijk, he announced; Children's Dyke. Near the confluence of the Lek and Noord Rivers, about fifteen kilometres east of Rotterdam. There are nineteen windmills roundabout, built over two hundred and fifty years ago to drain the marshes so that humans could settle and create a community. Humans regard this place as very special. Unique, in fact. It has special status in the world. I'd say we are very lucky to be here, to have this chance to see the famous windmills of Kinderdijk.

Dewei was squirming. Sorry to dampen your enthusiasm,

Teacher Chung, he began, but the fact is we're in the wrong place. We were supposed to go to Belgium.

So saying as he reached the lowest point of descent, Dewei hopped off, followed by the others.

As the sails whooshed and swung above them, the eight decamped en masse into the more reliably placid waters of the adjacent dyke. Belgium could wait, they decided. First, breakfast.

High above, Chii-nii waited. And then suddenly, for no good reason they could think of, she began to weep.

A LESSON IN EMOTIONS

She's crying, explained Chung. Her emotions are spilling over, out of her eyes.

Weird, thought the others. What were emotions?

Feelings, he continued, experiencing Chii-nii's tears as fine rain. The feeling I have for Lok because he is my son, but also the feelings I had for my partner, and the feelings I have now for all of you. The feelings I have about this trip. The feelings I have about my life and death. The feelings I have about all these feelings.

Bo was puzzled. Did she have feelings? Most of the time she simply felt numb. Or angry, but this was not a sensation she liked at all, so kept it under lock and key.

The others were not sure either. Cong knew he sometimes felt angry too; Dewei also. Lok and Shuang felt fear at their tails more often than not. While Hu-tu and Li Qin were in total agreement that the drakes had such a head start over them in just about everything that sometimes they feared their feathers would turn green with envy.

Chung looked up at the new female and begged her to come down and join them.

Please don't cry, he said. There's enough water around here already.

But when the others began to laugh at such an excellent joke,

Chii-nii began to weep even harder. They were all making fun of her, she choked. Could they not understand her extreme joy – the sense of relief – to have found them?

Sensibly, not really understanding joy and relief that manifested as tears, they all left her to it, and dabbled about feeding and enjoying the fresh loveliness of the morning.

Sorry, she apologized later, landing next to Chung. I get like that sometimes. It's such a weight, you see, carrying so much responsibility for trying to keep the world awake and turning. No-one understands ... Sometimes it's just too much.

Yes, you have quite a job, Chung agreed. Spinning nature into being, weaving strands of consciousness together, keeping the mill turning so that the stars continue their precessive drift through their grand cycle of golden through to dark ages. Quite a job.

Chung was in awe. He had found consolation in the clear imbalance of their group of eight being such an important number in mathematics, science, religion, culture, divination and superstition. In China, for example, the number eight was regarded as exceptionally lucky.

Now they were nine, he had no doubt that Chii-nii was the finely attuned sensitive they had been waiting to manifest; any skepticism as to the wisdom of the endeavour fell away. Finally they were one, on their way to being perfectly in balance.

Chii-nii was nodding. She could sense his river of thought. Which made her so happy she began weeping all over again.

That enchanting hen will drown in tears if she's not careful, thought Cong. And much to his surprise he felt his heart beat a little faster.

A LESSON IN SHADOWS

So are we going to Belgium or not? snapped Dewei. Lok had just beaten him to some late-developing frog spawn, and he felt an irritation out of all proportion.

Chii-nii advised not, which put Dewei in an even worse temper. His mood was like a dark cloud ... like the shadow that hung over Belgium, she teased without smiling, explaining that every country has its shadow side, some countries darker than others.

But it has the best mussels in the world, enthused Lok, not wanting to think about anything negative. And chocolate!

Also he had heard on his own epicurean grapevine that there was a café somewhere on the border where you could sit outside and drink coffee or hot chocolate in the Netherlands, then stand up, and step into Belgium. There were tiles on the pavement that read NL and B, and a demarcation line inbetween.

Sounds fun, he said. I'd like to see that.

Sharply, Chung ordered him to stop thinking of his stomach and pleasurable jaunts. The fact was that, having arrived in Kinderdijk, whether by accident or as part of some grand design, they no longer needed to go to Belgium to get to China.

Chii-nii nodded in agreement. She too thought they ought to simply head straight across Germany – a country that lay under the darkest of shadows, she knew, but at least they would save time.

Lok demurred. Dewei lightened up. Bo breathed a great sigh of relief for her sister and brothers. And so it was decided.

Despite Belgium's undoubted assets – shellfish and bittersweet stuff being only two of them – and despite it being so near, just over the border from Breda, such interesting destinations such as Antwerp, Bruges, Brussels and Maastricht were suddenly off their flight path, indeed off their world map.

Leipzig would be their next inland port of call, then Dresden, Prague and Vienna, avoiding the severely mountainous regions to the south, but still tough going all the same.

But first they would relax, talk through all differences and try to consolidate a collective strength. Three days, they decided; three days off before setting off.

Excuse me, but just one more thing, Bo asked as they began to disperse for their own particular versions of R & R. Why were we going to Belgium in the first place?

Because Teacher Chung had heard long ago of a colony of Mandarins there, replied Cong. He thought we might swing past, ask if any would like to come along.

Chii-nii knew of them, of course; her cobweb of connections spun far and wide, the threads of synchronicity she wove light but tight. Most of the Mandarins were still there, but being a pretty lazy bunch, they appeared – on the surface at least – to accept Belgium as their destiny.

It was their choice to stay, for better for worse, she reflected. She had hung out with them a while, tried to persuade a few of the more flexible and open-minded to accompany her.

In the end, she recalled, I was the only one who knew in my bones to come here. You could say that I'm the only survivor.

Germany

For small creatures such as we the vastness is bearable only through love.

Carl Sagan

As soon as they were airborne again, they felt the difference. With each duck moving forward to take the lead in rotation, and the others flying four by four behind in precise and faultless formation, it felt as if they were a single bird rather than nine.

Perfect, thought Chung with a deep sense of relief and gratitude. We fly as one, mindless … the only problem is that as soon as we land and are back in the world, our foolish minds will begin chattering and we'll be nine ducks with personal problems all over again.

Stop worrying, he heard Chii-nii instruct softly from her position just behind Cong.

All shall be well, and all shall be well, and all manner of things shall be well, she was murmering, quoting human words deeply lodged in the past.

Chung felt her words in his head rather than heard them by ear. Gentle words. Kind words. Duckepathic words that allowed his anxiety to dissipate, fade without regret into cloud and sky.

Once again he saw a feather – black, from Deiwei's tail – fall away, this time to be picked up by the wind and whisked away on ever playful air currents.

HOPS, SKIPS AND JUMPS

It was approximately two hundred kilometres between Dortmund to the north and Cologne to the south, then twice that distance again to the ancient trading city of Leipzig, which they accomplished in a series of seamless hops, skips and jumps that seemed almost too easy to be true.

Sometimes they flew during the day, at other times overnight, depending on the democratic decision of the group. Whenever they rested, they would discuss the next leg of the journey – how far, where to, and when.

It might depend on the weather. Though heading into summer, due to human intervention they could no longer rely on normal seasonal changes and climatic conditions.

There were heavy rains, dramatic changes in temperature, and even on one occasion, near Gottingen, a small but very surprising tornado that took all the Monday morning washing on an unexpected whirlwind tour of one particular village.

A petticoat ended up flying from the church spire. Several pieces of even more intimate underwear landed in the pond where the group of nine just happened to be resting after lunch. One of them wrapped itself around Dewei's head, which made them all laugh – except of course the duck blinded by a pair of large white bloomers!

Bo was nearly strangled by a scarlet thong. Lok took to wearing a lacy bra with alacrity, aided and abetted by Li Qin, who joined him in a duck dance that had onlookers applauding and shrieking with laughter.

It seemed that every time they stopped anywhere near human habitation, they swiftly drew a crowd. A few hurled stones, but most were appreciative, throwing bread and bits of leftover food, and even clapping as the ducks took off in their near seamlessly formed, arrow-shaped pattern of passage.

Having toured Leipzig and spent the night in the penguin pool at the zoo (the penguins all being locked up and therefore having no say in the matter, though they were very peeved to have missed such rare and illustrious visitors), the group moved on to Dresden.

They could see its especially dark shadow in the distance, for though the same size of Leipzig and rebuilt, its history was still too fresh, the suffering too extreme.

Can you believe it? Chung thought. Germany bombed Coventry, not far from where we met in middle England, and then England bombed Dresden in revenge.

What's a bomb? Bo wondered duckepathically.

A horrible weapon designed by people to hurt and kill other people, replied Chung, upon whom Cong, Dewei, Shuang, Hu-tu and Bo still depended for new information or to help them remember.

The beautiful ancient cathedral in Coventry was destroyed, so in retaliation, the beautiful ancient cathedral in Dresden was destroyed, he continued. German bombs killed over five hundred humans in Coventry; English bombs murdered around twenty-five thousand in Dresden.

The facts of such willful destruction and human misery weighed heavily on them as they flew over the city, even though it appeared superficially at least to be once again thriving and successful.

But because the vibrations of war still echoed, sinister and painful, not one of them wanted to stop, even for a minute.

Instead Chung offered a blessing, and Chii-nii wove a heart of peace and love and dropped it over Dresden in a tear-filled shower of empathy.

The Czech Republic

Ducks are strange animals.
The way they squat and squabble.
Sometimes they talk to you as if you
Understand what they saying...
And sometimes they are right.

Bill Murphy

Having sprung in the northeastern mountains of the Czech Republic, the River Elbe meandered its way into Germany and towards the sea.

It was sad to leave it, to head towards the Vltava on which Prague, the country's splendid capital, is situated.

River banks were craggy and forested one stretch, verdant and idling with cattle and horses another, or ranked with crops and burgeoning vines – grapevines! And wherever there were villages, there were gardens, and wherever there were gardens there was the scent of early roses and honeysuckle in profusion, rambling over fences, around walls and over roofs. It was, Chung claimed, so very, very rustic.

Lok disagreed. It was not that he thought rustic was the wrong word, it was just not sufficiently sensory. Surely bucolic described the scene so much better.

Look at it, he urged the others. Listen to it. Smell it. Touch it ...

Taste it? the others reminded him.

Taste it, Lok agreed, thinking it interesting that this sense had been last on his list, rather than first. Was he changing? Certainly he was slightly slimmer than when he set out, but was that all?

They bobbed about on the Vltava under the Charles Bridge, communing with the various waterfowl – who described themselves contrarily as stay-at-home bohemians – that had made this stretch of the river their own. Not one could understand why any bird would even want to fly up or down stream, let alone to China, a place that registered zilch in their geographic comprehension.

Prague was as fine a place as any, they reckoned. Finer perhaps. Constantly teeming with visitors, there was always something going on. Had the nine visited the castle? Or seen the famous clock? At that very moment, there were events all over the city as part of a Roma Festival.

Roma?

A tribe of humans that had left India many years before, wandering into Europe and creating entertainment along the way. They had always had to struggle to survive, with many humans critical of those who chose to stay on the move rather than settle down.

Humans are so peculiar, Cong said, shaking his head. Why can't they just live and let live, like us?

Because they think their way is right. But they only think this because they are so insecure and unsure deep down. It makes them blind. (This from a lone swan who had lost her mate to a careless cruiseboat captain and was bitterly sad.)

Yes, it all comes down to individuals and the egos they develop as children to protect them from the world. (This was an owl twit-twooing its own particular brand of homespun wisdom from one of the arches, and to whom Chung dipped his head in homage.)

Chung knew his personal limits, or rather he thought he did. Yes, he knew lots of stuff, but he was not so good at helping individuals overcome the personal baggage of their lives that prevented them from becoming the very best they could be.

Don't be so hard on yourself, advised the owl. It seems to me you're doing a pretty good job.

Me, scoffed Chung? I can teach, I can advise, but as a healer? Useless.

The illuminations on the bridge suddenly seemed much dimmer.

Chung hoped his eyes were not failing, but at his age anything was possible. Maybe he needed to find help. If not a healer, maybe a pair of glasses?

UP AND OVER

He would need more than a pair of glasses to get them all over the higher terrain that lay between the Czech Republic and Austria, he realized, looking ahead.

Chii-nii sensed his anxiety and moved closer. She was trying to merge with the group while not intruding, knowing the depth of relationship already existing among the others. She could feel the deep bond of kinship between Dewei, Shuang, Hu-tu, Bo and the handsome and fearless (if occasionally off-route) Cong – handsome in her eyes, at least.

She could sense the love between Lok and Li Qin, which appeared on the surface to be troubled but was in fact indestructible.

And she knew that Chung was beginning to doubt his ability to see the trip through.

Excuse me for interfering, she began gently. But have you thought about taking the bus? Or even a train?

Chung rocked on his heels – no mean feat for feet of the webbed variety.

Of course he had seen coaches on motorways, and trains on tracks all across England and Europe. But he had never once thought of taking advantage of them; for one thing he was not quite sure how. How could they so travel, where would they perch? Buses and trains were not like vans and cars; it was not so easy to hide away, especially these days with designs sleeker than ever.

Li Qin agreed that, with nine of them, maybe a bus would be difficult. And passenger trains went so fast that it might be hard to rest on top. One high-velocity swoosh through a tunnel and that would be the end of them for sure.

But how about a freight train? she suggested. Some have open cars. I'll check them out, and she went into a huddle with herself and made some duckepathic contacts with companies and timetables.

Good and bad news, she reported in no time at all.

The good news is there are lots of direct trains from two stations. The bad news is they are all fast and designed for passengers, not freight. Most goods between Prague and Vienna seem to go by air or road. I'm not sure how we could get aboard and stay hidden for the four-hour journey. As to riding outside, you're right: with no decks and carriages streamlined, they'd be no claw holds. We'd just slide off.

Could we hide underneath somehow?

We could try, but there are lots of tunnels through the mountains. And the fumes would be so bad we might suffocate.

The group bobbed about gravely. It appeared they had no choice but take to the wing again.

To lighten the mood and help take his father's mind off the uphill flight to come, Lok suggested a small side trip. It was not far, he assured them, just up and over the river to the foothills of the castle, in the Lesser Town or Little Quarter, known as Mala Strana.

They landed on the red-tiled roof of an ancient burgher house, which Lok told his excited mate had been used as a background location in several films and commercials.

Even though it was dark and late in the evening, Li Qin immediately began looking around for cameras. Maybe it was here in Prague that she would be spotted; after the disappointment of Rotterdam, she had felt quite desperate. Now she could be optimistic again.

See that building over there? Lok said, indicating from the top of the gable where they were perched: A splendid former monastery restored to the highest standard imaginable (or words to that effect, as quoted earlier by a human tourist standing by the bridge and reading from a brochure). It's a hotel.

There are hotels all over the place, noted Dewei. What's so special about this one?

Its name.

Oh, I see, said Chung, who was delighted to find he did not need glasses at all, at such a distance anyway. It's as far from home as we are.

The others looked at him quizzically. Would he please stop talking in riddles?

It's a Mandarin Oriental.

FROM MANDARINS TO STRAWBERRIES

It was just after dawn and they were standing on the top step of the hotel, having walked from just around the corner. Walking came as easy as flying, which is rare among ducks in general; Mandarins were blessed in so many ways, they agreed.

Have you ever seen anything so beautiful? breathed Li Qin.

Awesome, agreed Lok.

My, oh my, muttered Hu-tu to herself; I'd love to see the kitchen.

Just then the door swung open (for an early bird, Lok joked) and they beat a hasty retreat back into the shadows.

Well, now you can say you have seen a luxury hotel, noted Chung. It's a chain, you know (which of course they didn't.) That means there are several hotels with the same name. This is the Mandarin Oriental Prague, but the first was the Mandarin Oriental in Hong Kong.

Is Hong Kong in China? asked Cong, noting a similarity somehow in the sound of their names.

Well, it wasn't back then, but it is now, sort of. A long story … I'll fill you in later if you're interested.

It was time, Chung thought, for them to move on, and since the city was encircled with ring roads, he thought it best to fly to where they might pick up a lift before it got light. Hitchhiking was very common in this country, he knew, but he still crossed two claws for luck.

They flapped their way rather erratically (since several were half-asleep after the excitements of the night before) for several kilometres, and then perched in a tree alongside the two-lane road that led towards the mountains.

Keep watch for an open truck, ordered Cong. Stay quiet and get ready to go, go, go …

Which is how and why just before daybreak they found themselves in a fluttering heap among boxes and boxes of sweet-smelling strawberries.

Well, this is a surprise, whispered Chung. But rather apt: strawberries are fruit and so of course are we.

We are? chorused five ducks in a tangle of sibling rivalry to find the most comfortable position for the long drive ahead.

In many countries, there's a small citrus fruit that some call tangerines and in Japan, mikan. But its original name is mandarin. Mandarin oranges.

Mandarin ducks. Mandarin hotels. Mandarin oranges …

Whatever next? they wondered.

SANDLER AND MIGNONETTE

As the group woke periodically through the morning, they would catch snippets of conversation from the cab at the front of the truck. But of course the only person who understood was Chii-nii, and she was asleep much of the time.

If she had been able to understand Czech, Hu-tu would have heard the couple – a young man and woman, both with brightly coloured bandanas and wearing well-worn denim dungarees – talking about the load of organically grown fruit they were carrying to restaurants in Vienna.

The Sandlers are exceptional this summer, said the man with the blue bandana; we ought to get a really good price.

But you know me, replied the woman with a red bandana. I prefer the really intense taste of the little ones ... as close to wild strawberries as they can be, having been grown from seed! And think how pretty they'll sound on the menu: Mignonette.

Whenever the truck passed through tunnels, a light came on the cab. But even when the couple turned to check everything was alright in the back, they never saw a feather twitch. In fact they never even saw a hint of duck down.

When climbing steep inclines, the engine occasionally groaned. But on downhill runs, it sang as sweetly as the day itself: bright, warm and clear.

The group was getting hungry and thirsty, but even Lok managed to withhold complaint. They were in this adventure together, and that was that.

Soon after crossing the border into Austria the couple stopped for their own lunch, which they ate out of boxes on their laps. They then climbed out and walked into some trees, where they lay down and seemed all set for a nap.

Seeing their chance, the group hopped up onto the tailboard one by one and dropped off, down onto the road. They thought they would just take a minute or two to forage and find some water, but found themselves by necessity straying further and further from the truck.

It was Cong who heard it start up first.

Yikes, he screeched, run!

But they were all too late. Even though they had chosen to live a slow life, the nice couple and their eco load had moved on. After all, as Chung later reflected pragmatically, fresh fruit did not stay fresh for long.

Austria

You can know the name of a bird in all the languages of the world, but when you're finished, you'll know absolutely nothing whatever about the bird... So let's look at the bird and see what it's doing – that's what counts. I learned very early the difference between knowing the name of something and knowing something.

Richard P. Feynman

Now what do we do? It's all your fault, Bo, charged Dewei. You're so dopey. I could have jumped on in time but you were so slow.

Bo hung her head. She felt awful. But the truth was she could not run as fast as the others. The nice animal doctor in Compton had made her wing perfect for flight, but there was still something not quite right when on the ground. Not that she limped exactly. It was more subtle than that.

Oh stop it, interjected Cong, springing to his sister's defence. Lok was just as bad, pigging out by the stream.

To which, of course, Li Qin reacted like a lioness defending her family, screaming at Cong and sideswiping Bo with her wing.

With the group disintegrating into blame and panic, it was Chii-nii who heard singing in the distance, lifted her head and began to voice in harmony.

One by one they stopped quarrelling as the music became louder and more and more entrancing. And then they saw them coming: a line of motorized caravans, some of which had decks on the back on which sat humans of all shapes and sizes and wearing all the colours of the rainbow, clapping hands and singing.

Perfect, said Chii-nii. Roma.

Those Roma who first saw the group of ducks exclaimed in surprise and admiration to find such pretty things on the side of the road. Where could they have come from? Where could they be going?

Would you like to come with us? asked a bright-eyed smiling girl with dark eyes and equally dark hair in a thick glossy braid down her back. I'm sure we can find room.

Chung was not sure. It all depended on where – or rather in which direction – the Roma were heading.

Chii-nii read his mind, then in turn read that of the girl's father, generously endowed with a handsome moustache and the unofficial leader of the group, just as Chung was the unofficial leader of his own.

It's good, Chii-nii gee-geed to the others. The travellers are going around Vienna, where people are less tolerant than in Prague, and then on to Hungary.

Hungary? misinterpreted Lok. I most certainly still am.

AN EVEN SLOWER LIFE

There were five families, all related, each with their own living and travelling quarters beautifully decorated with lace and embroidery, with all mod cons: toilet, kitchen, TV and mobile WiFi. Well over a dozen adults, including mothers and fathers and grandparents, uncles and aunts, and near twenty children, all packed in at night like sardines in a can but perfectly comfortable and happy.

They had been at the Roma festival, of course, and were now – sedately, in their own style of slow life way – en route to Hungary.

You would have loved the procession in Prague, the girl told the ducks, at least one of whom she sensed understood every word; there were Roma from all over the world, even India!

She had ordered two young cousins off a deck to make room for their new fellow-travellers, and it was a lesson in hospitality for certain members of the group of nine that the boys moved so willingly, with smiles rather than complaints.

The children went off quite happily to pluck grasses to act as bedding, which quickly made the Mandarins feel at home. The group could perch on the rails during the day, jumping back down if vehicles behind caused trouble by hooting or shouting out of windows.

For the large part though, Chii-nii swore, they were totally safe; she had knowledge of Roma people and knew that this group's heart was one hundred per cent in the right place.

Music is a great leveler, she said. Don't you agree, Li Qin? You're going to have a wonderful time, dancing and singing to your own heart's content.

But first the caravan of vehicles had to circumnavigate Vienna, with such crowds on the ring roads that there were traffic jams virtually the whole way. By experience, the Roma travellers knew not to stay together and create hostility among impatient drivers; instead they separated, only coming together at night in a lay-by or on the verge.

In general the public was not friendly. Farmers denied access to land and water. Police tried to move them on. But they had been roaming the route for years – over countless lifetimes in fact – and knew where to stop for acceptance and help.

Beyond Vienna, life became less stressful; order was created from potential chaos, and soon enough the Group of Nine were crossing yet another border.

Hungary

With a bit of luck
A duck
Will come into your life.
When you are at the peak
Of your great powers
And your achievement towers
Like a smoking chimney stack.
There'll be a quack,
And right at your feet
A little duck will stand.
She will take you by the hand
And lead you,
Like a child with no defence;
She will lead you
Into wisdom, joy and innocence.
That little duck.
We wish you luck.

Michael Leunig

When the caravan stopped, their new friend and supporter, Nadya, a Romani name that means hope, would come and make sure they could find water and food. She would also check the group was fully aboard before the vehicles set off again.

When travelling, Nadya would sit close by, either outside or in, with a book and read. She finished one book before they even reached Gyor. Chii-nii said it was one of Nadya's grandmother's favourites as a girl, having deepened her knowledge of Hungary's history. It told of how tribes called the Huns and later the Magyars swept into Europe from Eurasia, a re-telling of the legendary story of Atilla using the mystical image of a white stag.

Dewei clucked in disapproval; everyone knew that like unicorns, white stags were mythical and not real. Why would such an obviously intelligent young woman waste her time on such fancies?

Well, that's where you are wrong, Chii-nii replied gently. Because I have met several white unicorns and stags, and they are very real, especially to those who allow themselves to believe. Life can be very mysterious, you know, if you allow it to be.

You know, said Dewei the following day when they were well on their way into Hungary: I think Chii-nii has put a spell on us. I can think of no other explanation as to why we are travelling like this. I mean, we're ducks, not gypsies.

We're ducks hitching a lift with gypsies, corrected Shuang, who was really enjoying watching the world go by, and liked hearing Nadya reading aloud, even if he didn't understand a word of the language in which it was written.

But we could be flying up the Danube, which goes all the way to Budapest. There's even a hydrofoil …

The others looked between the two brothers, who normally did not argue. Or rather Dewei would try to and Shuang always caved in.

We could put it to a vote, said Bo, sensibly. That's the best way.

So they tried to vote, but there were too many abstentions: Chung (who claimed academic immunity), Chii-nii (who felt that as a spinner and weaver of life she was far too busy), Bo (because she was the youngest and least sure of herself, even though it was all her idea), and Shuang (who backed down and said he didn't really mind either way).

Honestly, sighed Cong. What a lot we are. Well, I guess that means we just carry on, go with the flow. And look, we're coming into Gyor, which has lots of hotsprings; that has to be good news. Let's all calm down, forget our differences. Remember, united we stand, divided we fall …

While paddling like crazy just to stay where we are, and not drown, added Lok, breaking the deadlock of discomfort with a jokey mime to illustrate the point.

Or die of boredom, sighed Li Qin, who really fancied having a knees up. Here she was, surrounded by Roma talent, and with no apparent chance to show off her own.

PERFORMER IN THE SPOTLIGHT

The opportunity came that evening, after splashing about in the numerous brooks and different pools of medicinal warm water that Nadya led them to on the outskirts of the town.

One was so comforting to Bo that she decided to spend the night there, paddling around, flexing her legs and wings, or simply resting. From that moment on, Nadya could do no wrong in Bo's eyes; she had to be a nearly perfect human.

Within Li Qin's belief system, however, she herself was the perfect all-round singing/dancing/performing Mandarin duck. And that evening, when the caravan welcomed people of all ages, shapes and sizes from the vicinity to listen to stories and enjoy music around a campfire, she held nothing back.

It was an impromptu session, celebrating a scattering of birthdays and the many blessings of a semi-nomadic creative life. Tales were told. Beer was passed around. Instruments tuned. Babies fed on the breast and lulled to sleep.

When the musicians finally began to play and the dancers to dance – Hungarian verbunkos, which began slowly but became faster and faster – Li Qin quivered with excitement, jumped up and immediately began to twirl with the crowd ... but far out on the edge, just in case she got stamped on.

Lok egged her on, gee-geeing encouragement. The others too, but he of course had a special interest.

And the more attention Li Qin received – Look, look, a duck dancing! Oh my, and singing! (or trying to sing!) – the more effort she summoned up, concentrating her energies to please the crowd.

Some of the younger men had guitars or fiddles. Nadya's father (who had waxed his handsome moustache for the occasion) played the accordion, her sweetheart of a mother a small drum.

As for Nadya, she squeezed and fingered an Argentine bandonean with such panache and tossed her head so violently in time and tune to the music that Hu-tu in particular feared it might fall off.

Many of the older folk – men and women – used sticks to tap out the rythmns on the ground, grunting in time to the music and vocally imitating the instruments. Not only was the sound unique but so infectious that soon everyone was on their feet.

It was a genuine fusion of old and new, Nadya explained to the crowd, quite out of breath from her favourite musical exertion. Traditionally Roma did not play instruments. Now some were even experimenting with jazz – a forbidden if not unheard of genre not so long ago.

With so many people stamping and shouting, twisting and turning, the fire shot streams of sparks into the sky. The older ones tired first, of course, and as the night drew on, one by one the dancers withdrew, sinking to the ground in a state of ecstatic exhaustion or leaving for home.

Finally, only Nadya's father and Nadya herself were left playing, pulling out all the stops in honour of the one small figure still quodelling, hip-hopping, and turning in circles: Li Qin, in her element, having the time of her life.

MORE WINDMILLS?

Exhausted, the dancing duck slept late, and woke to find the caravan on its way again, with only one more stop – Tata, just a few miles from Tatabanya – where they would stay until it was time to head for the next festival …

Oh, she croaked, having all but shredded her vocal cords the night before. Are those Hungarian windmills?

She was peering out into the distance, to where what appeared to be hundreds of white sails were turning.

Not exactly, it's a Hungarian wind farm, Lok said, comforting her gently with his beak, as if to say, There, there dear ... I know everything hurts but really you only have yourself to blame. It's the price a star must pay …

Turbines, machines that create energy from wind, elaborated Cong.

But wind is energy, Bo corrected. That doesn't make sense.

Following a similar line of thought, it didn't make sense to Nadya either, to create energy from energy.

But that's humans for you, she murmered sadly, unable to shrug off a nagging sense of deep bewilderment and adolescent disillusion with her own kind.

TIME OUT

It was a nice place where the caravan halted for several weeks. Tata stood beside a beautiful lake, which quickly proved the perfect environment for the ducks.

Li Qin swiftly recovered to perform over and over again, and soon people were coming from far and wide to see the little Mandarin go through her theatrical paces. They even gave her a nickname, Shirley, after Shirley Maclaine, who proved to be as popular in Hungary as she was everywhere else ... not that Li Qin (or Shirley for that matter) had a clue, but funny all the same.

Chung was happy to simply be. He was tired. Desperately

tired. But he could not admit so to any of the others, even Lok. Especially Lok. After all, he didn't want to be a burden to any member of the group, especially his own son.

I will just keep quiet and struggle on, he kept telling his self. Only when I get to China, then maybe I can let go ... But I have to get there. I have to see China with my own eyes. I have to reach home.

The group grew as fond of the Roma as the Roma loved them. Trust was implicit and every night both sides thanked the gods for such a meeting of kindred spirits: creatures that liked to keep on the move but were not averse to a restorative rest stop every so often.

Believe me, stated Nadya's father, fingering his moustache with feeling. You won't want to spend a day more than you have to on the festival venue sites. We love the music, but as for the rest ... crazy. Enjoy the peace and quiet while you can.

The days grew longer and time all but stopped. Water lapped tree-clad banks and the stones of ancient fortifications. Leaves and flowers matured. Bees buzzed. The sun shone hot and strong.

The Mandarins had begun to moult, properly lose their feathers, so the timing could not have been better.

Then one day in early July, they were on the move again, heading not eastwards to Budapest as might be expected, but south by back roads to Lake Balaton.

WORLD MUSIC

The ducks learned a lot about the world and world music that summer.

First the caravan spent a week on the south bank of the largest freshwater lake in Europe, playing music day and night to thousands upon thousands of young humans from all over the world. It was unutterably shocking to the group of nine, who paddled off the moment they arrived and stayed undercover until Nadya signaled it was safe to emerge and time to go.

But it was never boring. One evening, hidden beneath a fringe of willow, Chung told them about a historic wall named after Berlin to keep East and West apart. For some reason, relatives and friends separated by this wall could meet at Lake Balaton and spend precious time together. It was only a few years before he was born that this wall had come down, reuniting Germany.

Another time Chii-nii taught them the name Mandarin in the languages of the countries they had travelled through so far: mandarijneend in Dutch; mandarinente in German; kachinka mandarinska in Czech; mandarinrece in Hungarian.

And in preparation for future travels, mandarinka for Russia, yuanyang for China, and maybe oshidori for Japan.

Why Japan? asked Hu-tu.

Because a good third of our tribe hang out there, some of whom nationalistically choose to believe they are indigenous to Japan, not China. The rest may like to consider returning home.

Dewei looked askance. He saw no point in going further than they had to. As far as he was concerned, China was as far as he was going, and not one kilometre or mile more.

There again he had great respect for Chii-nii. Indeed it was a complex emotion that was rather more than simple respect, but embarrassed, he decided – for once – to stay silent. Not that he thought he had a chance with a goddess, but then if Cong could assume she was interested, why not he?

Being rather more direct if not straightforward, Bo wanted to know about mating, about which Cong and Dewei cringed, Lok and Li Qin looked knowing, Shuang and Hu-tu felt stirrings of curiosity, and Chii-nii shook with heart-swelling emotion.

Well, began Chung, when you choose your partner, you have strong feelings of affection and desire. You will want to become as close as possible and at the moment of greatest excitation and thrill become as one, with no separation. This is the moment at which procreation occurs.

Procreation?

You create young ones together. You females lay fertilized eggs and, once hatched, you males look after your families while the females are busy. You will find out next year, when spring comes around again.

Dewei looked concerned. As for Cong, his frustration was so acute that he had to paddle furiously to reduce his stress.

Do we have to wait so long?

To meet other Mandarin ducks ready for mating, yes. There are no free drakes here, pointed out Chung. After all, Lok is taken and as for you hens ...

Hu-tu felt sad. With a soft and sentimental heart (in combination with the ambition to repopulate the world) she would have liked to start a family months ago.

Bo was not bothered. Being rather lazy by nature, she could wait.

As for Chii-nii, there was just too much spinning and weaving to be done before she could even begin to think about next year.

What about each other? asked Shuang, and was immediately splashed and pelted with water by his brothers and sisters for coming up with such a nonsensical idea.

They were not sure why they felt so strongly that he had crossed some unacceptable line. Until the next session, that is, when Chung explained the basics of genetics.

NO DUCK IS AN ISLAND

August found them in Budapest, on an island in the river between the East and West banks. The Obudai-Sziget festival was another massive gathering of musicians and music buffs from all around the globe.

For the first time in their lives, the group of nine were made aware of Finns and Cubans, Africans and Mexicans, Indians and Argentines, Mongolians and Balinese, Aboriginal people from Australia, First Nationers from the Americas, and Celts from

Ireland. They even saw Chinese, said to be travelling in larger numbers than ever; it was all so exciting.

As for the music, Nadya explained, it was the chance to play with musicians from different cultures and traditions. Her parents had attended the very first WOMAD festival years before she was even born, and had returned home fired with enthusiasm: intercultural experimentation was not only exciting but took music to a new level: it was a universal language, proving that the world was one.

That is when her family had started touring, following events far and wide rather than just drifting around on a nomadic whim or following well-worn ancient tribal tracks and ley lines.

Again the ducks tried as hard as possible to keep out of sight, this time by roosting in the trees overlooking the narrower part of the river of the island. While closer to development, including a rail track and bridges, vegetation was thicker here than on other parts of the island which was once a shipyard, and indeed from above was shaped like a ship!

Being mid-August, it proved too hot and humid to do anything but feed and doze, bob about under overhanging branches on the wash of passing boats, and dream, while listening to music that was wild one moment, sobbing the next, and always demanding attention. Listen, it seemed to say; listen to our stories, listen to what we have to say ...

Listening at dusk one evening to the eerie but inspirational tones of Mongolian tuva throat singing in combination with Indonesian percussion, the ducks were startled when Nadya appeared below them, gazing upwards to where they were gathered on an especially hospitable forked branch.

Hey, she called to no-one in particular. Guess what? A friend wants to say hello.

Hello, said a young man's voice, and a second face upturned.

Cong, Dewei, Shuang, Hu-tu and Bo could not believe their eyes.

It was the young musician from Compton. It was Jim.

COINCIDENCE OR SYNCHRONICITY?

When they thought about, it didn't seem so crazy to meet Jim so far from where they had first met. After all, he was a musician, and a musician with a very open mind. Also they knew he had no fear of travelling. Nor of colouring his hair, which was now blue.

But for Jim to run across them five months on with a group of Roma in Hungary of all places, well ... he admitted to having no words to express his astonishment. Yet it was because of Cong, Dewei, Shuang, Hu-tu and Bo that he was at the festival: the song he had written about them had launched his career, and now he had an agent and was recording and selling music as fast as he could write it.

Luckily, I met Nadya on the campsite, he explained, as if they understood every word. She was listening to me play on a side stage and invited me to go and jam with her family. Thank goodness she knows a few words of English, otherwise I would never have known you were here.

In the old days I would have thought it a series of amazing coincidences, he added thoughtfully. Now I know it's synchronicity.

It seems that when Jim told her that his father was a vet, Nadya told him about a group of Mandarin ducks hitch-hiking a ride.

Mind you, he continued, I was surprised when she said there were nine of you, not five. How did that happen, I wonder.

He also told them of something amazing that had happened back on the reservoir in Shropshire. How pure white lotus flowers had broken the surface and were blooming in all directions ... covering the surface in great beauty.

Anything to do with you? he enquired, smiling.

Jim was going to join the Roma for another month of smaller musical events into the autumn. He might then go home, but there again he might just ask to stay ... There was no way he was going to leave Nadya, he said. She was the one: the only one. And if that meant moving with the family to their winter quarters in

Szentendre, and staying there until the following Spring, then that is what he would do.

It was all very romantic. Lok and Li Qin began beaking. Chii-nii wondered if both Cong and Dewei had their eyes on her, which while pleasant enough could be problematical. Chung remembered his partner and wanted to die. And the five siblings sighed and sighed and sighed until a passing grebe told them to shut up and get a grip.

By the time Jim and Nadya had withdrawn to return to camp, the ducks' softly pleasurable gee-geeing sounded almost like purring.

AN IMPORTANT DECISION

The next day was the last day, and after one final spectacular concert, with amazing lighting effects and fireworks, the masses – musicians and fans alike – split in every direction, leaving an army of volunteers to clear up.

By the following evening, the island was quieter and the ducks could come out of hiding to be reunited with Jim, Nadya and all their other Roma friends.

Chung made sure only one small thing was felt behind: a tiny green feather cast from the top of Shuang's head that soon became indistinguishable from the vegetation all around.

What now? wondered Hu-tu, who had finally – after weeks of waiting for an invitation – been given a tour of the caravans' kitchens. Was something coming to an end? A door closing ...

It will be autumn soon, replied Chung. Our flight feathers are regrown, and while it's been very pleasant to potter around like this, I'm afraid we have to get serious. Do you realize how far we have travelled? Not far at all. From here, it's still a long way to China – ten, twenty times further than we have come already – and right now I'm thinking we need to let a train take the strain.

Conjuring up memories of freight trains and timetables, Chii-nii coughed politely.

From my research I believe there is only one rail company that can help us, she noted: The Trans-Siberian.

WHICH WAY?

Trying to gain a consensus as to the best route proved very trying. At one point Chung simply flew away and perched on the leading caravan in the convoy until he had recovered. It pained him to witness so much dissent, especially among individuals who normally were so reasonable and sensible.

Nadya had told Chii-nii that ahead the countryside would flatten out after they left Budapest, and that whether they went north or south all they would see for days would be a vast sky above a vast plain stretching ahead: the Puszta. And that was just the start of a journey that could take what felt like forever...

So as Chii-nii told the group, they had to take the train. There was Chung to consider; he was game but struggling. Also they needed to reach China before the first snow; they would need to find Yuanyang Lake to settle in to for winter.

Yuanyang (Mandarin) Lake? Where was that?

Nearer to Shanghai than Peking, so still a long way to go even after the Trans-Siberian track terminates.

But now, NOW, shouted Cong, who wanted to punch Dewei on his blind spot of a beak and tell Hu-tu and Li Qin to get down off their pedestals. Which way are we going NOW? Why are we talking about China when we are still thousands of miles away? If we're going to take a train, let's take a train ...

But northeast or southeast? Shuang dithered, unsure.

If we need to be north, why are we in Hungary? Bo mused.

Exactly. But if we go southeast ...

As Nadya said, it could take forever, broke in Chii-nii, and some of us may not make it. For one thing, some of the countries we'd fly over are in trouble. I think it would be best to steer clear of anywhere in conflict.

What about the Silk Road? Lok threw in for good measure, adding the further complication of still having to decide which of its three ancient trading routes to follow: north, south or right through the middle.

Chi-nii shook her head. They all had their difficulties, especially the central route that would take them smack bang through Tibet.

The Himalayas are no joke, she said firmly. I'm sure Chung would much rather freight to Kiev and then join the Trans-Siberian across to Ulan-Batar and then down to Beijing.

So you're suggesting we go north and then turn east? Dewei shrieked, beside himself with rage. I mean, how much time have we wasted!

Lok was indignant. What time have we wasted? Why, it's been a marvellous adventure so far. One thing different and we would not be here now ...

Here now, arguing, interjected Shuang, picking up the thread. I mean you're right, but oh brother!

The squabbling continued until they were all tired and bored with going round and round in circles. Deflated, they sat, sunk in gloom, either sulking or wishing they were somewhere else.

SAYING GOODBYE

Several hours later, in darkness, Chung returned from his retreat armed with clarity and a new resolve: The problem as he saw it was that they had become too attached to humans.

We have become dependent on them, following them. This is not going to help us any longer.

We need to say goodbye and thank you and start thinking for ourselves again, he continued. We are, after all, wild ducks. Jim's father knew that; however much he helped us, he always kept that in mind. Now we have forgotten that fact ourselves.

As the others listened attentively, they felt their hearts slow and their minds become calm.

We will not fly upriver to Szentendre, however enticingly beautiful the Danube Bend. Nor will we go north. Instead we will turn east to Tisza and then head for Odessa.

What?

Seven heads turned one to another, back and forth, startled.

Lok had wanted to see Szentrendre's pretty town square, with its cafes. Maybe check out the coffee?

You and coffee, teased Bo.

Cong had hoped to see the small medieval town of Visegrad with its castle.

Dewei wondered if they knew that Esztergom had the largest basilica in all Hungary. Not to be missed, for sure.

But there again, Chung was right. They were not tourists. Cafes, castles and churches really were irrelevant for ducks. Still ...

Everyone was so confused. Even Chii-nii appeared nonplussed.

I thought you wanted to take the train?

Chung regarded her gravely. Taking the train was initially her idea, he reminded her, thanking her for the concern that led to that decision and so much hard work. But it was clear to him they needed to fly east, with no distractions.

I feel so much better, he assured. It was losing myself in the human way that made me sink, feel so dispirited. Now that my energy has changed I'm ready to go.

For the first time in weeks, everything was crystal clear.

LESSON LEARNED

Leaving the Danube was a wrench, but the flight across the wide open spaces of the Puszta to Tisza and its lake, bordered by ancient stands of oak trees, proved to the group than that they could do a lot more than merely still flap their wings.

They all realized to a greater or lesser degree that their time with the Roma had taught a hugely important lesson. It was seductive to hang out and do little but indulge and be indulged.

But it did not move them forward with purpose in the same way as flying.

Now they had their focus back – China – and it felt good.

Chung felt completely revitalised.

Cong looked ahead to the challenge with clear eyes.

Dewei tried hard to be fair. .. to remember not to judge other individuals or the rest of the group at large but accept, accept, accept.

Shuang was so cheerful that he considered trying to get his facial muscles to smile in human fashion. But then he remembered that he was not a pet; he was a Mandarin, and only happy when all the others were happy, it was as simple as that.

Hu-tu worried that Chung was not as fit as she imagined he imagined.

Bo was stuck in resentment, and could only grunt in a passive-aggressive manner when any of the others tried to communicate. She had so wanted to stay in one place and never move again.

Lok and Li Qin were at peace.

As for Chii-nii, she thanked the energetic bond that bound them all together. For the first time for ages she felt she could tie a knot in the threads of their nine disparate personalities and have confidence that it would for the time being at least hold firm.

OUT OF THE MIST

The southern end of the lake proved a great feeding ground, and they gorged in anticipation of trials to come. Only the faint echoes of motorboats and water skiing to the north kept them on the tips of their claws.

It was a relatively new man-made lake but, as Chung said, it felt ancient and was rich in wildlife, with frogs hopping among waterlilies and some two hundred different kinds of birds. It was therefore – all things being equal – only a matter of time before they bumped into more ducks of their own kind.

It was dawn on the second day when Hu-tu – always an early

riser – flew down from her perch to start feeding and had the shock of her life.

Moving towards her through early morning mist off the surface of the lake were five pairs of Mandarin ducks.

Hu-tu turned to check that her own group was still intact, and then looked back at what she thought had to be some kind of mirage.

But no, there they were, purposefully paddling, two by two by two by two by two ... as nature intended.

Teacher Chung, she voiced softly. Goddess Chii-nii ... we have company.

As one by one the others awoke and peered out towards this apparent mirror image of themselves, they voiced first amazement and then concern.

Where had the group of ten come from? Were there more of them? Where were they going?

It was Chung and Chi-nii who swam out to make overtures. As they sounded a friendly approach, the group began gee-geeing their own excitement as they recognized Chi-nii.

Soon enough, she was introducing them as Mandarins she had known in Belgium.

I am astonished, she admitted. I never thought any of them would follow me. But it seems these five young pairs of brothers and sisters from two different sets of parents felt a strong enough urge to set out to catch me up.

But how did they know we were here? asked Bo.

Is it important? Chii-nii enquired gently. They are here, and now we must decide what to do next.

One of the new male Mandarins quickly interrupted. Now that they had found Chii-nii, they had their own plan. A familiar plan as it turned out: to head north and jump a freight train to Kiev and then hitch a ride all the way across Siberia and Mongolia to Beijing.

We are heading for the lake at the back of the Forbidden City, he said decisively. That is where we feel our ancestors must have originated. We have done our research.

Chii-nii looked alarmed. Not a good idea, she was sure of that. Too many people, too much pollution, no nature. But the bossy leader ignored her advice. He knew best.

We just wanted to pay our respects, he added, dipping his head first to Chii-nii and then to Chung the elder. And to thank you for the idea you planted so fruitfully. We will see you in China then.

Chung moved forward a little to ask gently why they were going to China.

Why? The group of ten voiced between themselves for some time and seemed unable to come to an agreement.

To see the world, said one.

To give our offspring a better chance in life, said another.

For the adventure ... to understand family roots ... for work (work?) ... to get rich ...

Seven of the nine looked at the ten with amazement.

To get rich? What on earth did this mean?

But the imperious leader of the Group of Ten was not interested in discussion. He just wanted to get going. So without wasting another minute in what he considered idle chat, they did.

The five couples swam back out into the open water and took off in a sudden noisy spray that, shot through with sunshine, fell back among the water lilies in a shower of rainbows.

DISTURBED

Cong, Dewei, Shuang, Hu-tu, Bo, Lok and Li Qin huddled together. Chung set himself apart and Chii-nii meditated on a branch high above the rest.

That brief encounter had upset them all.

Deciding it was best to continue as planned, they set off again as soon as Chung and Chii-nii rejoined the group. The lake was lovely and in many ways a splendid place to settle down, but as Chung reminded them, China was the place to be.

It was like a magnet, attracting all things Chinese back to their place of origin. For years Chinese people had emigrated and made lives all over the world, but now their children and their childrens' children were being drawn back to China and its economically exploding cities to find jobs and claim their heritage.

Making money is important to all humans, he explained. But making money to the Chinese is paramount; what might appear to an outsider to be greed is rooted historically in centuries of basic survival.

There are one-point-three billion humans in China, he added, and they all want to do better than their parents and grandparents. They all want success. They all want to be rich.

There was that word again. But what exactly did it mean?

Rich, murmered Chii-nii thoughtfully ... To be rich means to be wealthy. But wealth can mean so many things: food, health, happiness. Sadly for many it now means acquisitions, things, objects, to make them feel secure and comfortable.

And the very wealthy like to own things that they feel make them special and somehow better than and more important than – above – everyone else.

Within the last decade, Chung continued, ancient Chinese things, mostly stolen and taken all over the world in previous centuries, have been returning to China at the most amazing prices. Chinese are paying astronomical sums of money to buy back their history and traditional culture.

For example, he said, just the year before an ink-brush painting of lotus flowers and Mandarin ducks by a famed Chinese master had sold in Hong Kong for one hundred and ninety-one million HK dollars.

Is that a lot? asked Bo. It sounds like it might be.

Well, it is an enormous amount of money by human standards, Chung replied. Because of such prices, Chinese buyers are travelling all over the world, trying to find artifacts to take home and make their own fortunes.

Just recently, he added – now a fund of up-to-date information as much as academic knowledge – a blue-and- white charger with a design of Mandarin ducks from the Yuan Dynasty was put up for sale, also in Hong Kong. I don't know how much it cost, but you can be pretty sure it is now on mainland China, adding so-called value to someone's portfolio.

I think we are rich, said Hu-tu, surprising them all. We have food, water, beautiful feathers and strong bones, and one another. I mean, really, what else could we possibly need?

Ah well, this is where humans have become confused, Chung agreed, shaking his beak. They confuse need with want. Hu-tu, is there nothing you want but don't necessarily need?

A mate, and lots of ducklings, she replied, quick as a flash.

A charger of delicious slugs with acorns on the side, woo-wooed Lok, nudging his partner who looked embarrassed in admitting she wanted just about everything.

I want to fly, said Cong.

So do I, added Dewei.

So let's fly, concluded Chung, now that the discursive lecture was over. Carpathian Mountains, up, up and away ...

Romania

Mandarin ducks mate for life and will die of loneliness if separated from their chosen mate.

Katherine Paterson

For miles the plain stretched ahead, open, green and verdant, with farms and ranches and horses roaming wild and free. Then slowly it began to fold and shape as ahead, hills and mountains began to rise and fall.

Just before nightfall the second day, there was a cry from the rear to stop, stop.

Lok, who happened to be flying last, had become aware that they were being followed. He had felt it, he told the others after landing, and indeed, looking back saw four and a half pairs of Mandarins chasing after them.

You were right, we were wrong, the lone female wept. We were waiting for a train and some humans chased us with dogs and sticks, and the sticks made a dreadful noise and my mate fell down, closed his eyes and could not voice or fly again.

Yes, please, let us come with you, the others pleaded. Chii-nii, we beg your forgiveness.

Nothing to forgive, replied Chii-nii, making Hu-tu responsible for providing a feathered shoulder for the widowed Mandarin to cry on, and then conferring with Chung as to how best proceed. Quickly they agreed they needed to move on, not as if nothing had happened, but to avoid shock and disillusion setting in.

Just stay in the rear, she advised the nine newcomers. We will take the strain until you have recovered from the trauma of losing your friend.

And so eighteen ducks took off into the unknown with Chung in the lead and Hu-tu and Bo in charge of the female, who was inconsolable even on the wing, more than ready to give up her own ghost if it meant being with her partner again.

MILES AND MILES

From Oradea, they flew up a pass to Cluj Napoca, crossed some less difficult territory to reach Targu Mures and then rested awhile. From here they followed the River Mures and then tackled the last high range over to the county of Bacau.

Are we still in Hungary? asked Bo, gasping from altitude sickness as she landed on wobbly legs.

No, we left Hungary long ago, replied Cong, encouraging her with a friendly pat of his wing. Now we're in Romania, with the border into Moldavia straight ahead. Two hundred or so more miles and we'll reach Odessa.

Is that good?

It's a huge port on the Black Sea, which is always crowded with oil tankers, so it will be different for sure. Then across water to Crimea – over-shadowed by a large black cloud of its own – and then across more water into Georgia, another far from happy place.

Does that mean we are nearly there? asked Shuang.

'Fraid not, replied Lok, who was revelling in his reduced waistline but as hungry as hell. Another few days and I think we may be about halfway.

Only halfway, groaned Li Qin. I wish we were back with the Roma. They were so much more fun. I mean, this new lot of ducks have no gumption and can hardly say boo to a goose.

But they have flown all this way pursuing a dream, my dream, Chii-nii responded with feeling. I admire them for that. Let us be kind and lead them on, offering as much support as we can muster.

And then she suggested a ceremony to mark the passing of the overly bossy Mandarin, that had been so unkindly brought down by a hunter thinking (unwisely) to have duck for dinner.

At the base of a mossy tree, Chii-nii pushed dead leaves and bark aside with beak and claws to create a small circular space. She then asked the others to each gather a wild flower, leaf, blade of grass or bug and lay them one by one within the circle.

This is to celebrate the life of our dear brother and to help him on his way with beauty, water and food, Chii-nii said quietly, then threw back her head and keened to the rising moon. Soon all eighteen birds were voicing in unison, some remembering others who had passed, and others wondering about what it meant, exactly, to be killed and to die.

Afterwards, more than one said they were sure they had seen the shadow of a Mandarin passing overhead.

But the young female did not follow ... Rather she felt that having partially put his memory to rest – they had only been together for one season with no ducklings to cement their relationship – she could start again.

Russia

What's a duck's favourite dance? The quackstep.

Anon.

Four days later by the Gregorian calendar they were resting on the river Kuban, just outside Krasnodar.

Today is the last day of August, noted Dewei. Tomorrow it will be September ...

And autumn, Cong noted, his internal radar already plotting a flight path along the northern edge of the Caucasus to the Caspian Sea. There was still such a long way to go, but no way around the problem: they could only keep heading eastwards as swiftly as they could.

Remember, he said, with words of encouragement, we Mandarins don't migrate as we used to. So we are doing really well. Remarkably well.

But I need a break, pleaded Li Qin. You have no idea how hard this is for me. I'm creative, not sporty.

So entertain us, Chung ordered sagely.

Which led Li Qin to perform a spirited Cossack dance on the river bank that proved hugely entertaining all round. Some small children – members of Russian families fishing and enjoying picnics to celebrate the end of summer – joined in, laughing and shouting and stamping and have a fine old time.

Afterwards she felt so much better. They all did. Even the lone female began talking about when they got to China, and how maybe she could start life anew.

Shuang was very interested in such a rapid recovery. She was obviously very strong and courageous, and really rather pretty.

PREPARE TO DUCK

Crossing the Caspian Sea was the most testing part of the journey yet. It was such a wide stretch of water, and then there were its mysteries …

Decreed to be a sea by ancient Romans on their colonial march because it tasted salty, the largest landlocked inland lake in the world remains especially odd in being fed from the north by two freshwater rivers.

And then there was the monster.

Shuang, Lok, Hu-tu and Bo were all agog. They remembered Jim telling them about a monster nicknamed Nessie that lived in a Scottish lake or loch: could this be a relative?

The Caspian Sea Monster, laughed Dewei, who knew all about it.

Fifty years before, when the Caspian Sea was still within the borders of the Soviet Union, American spy satellites photographed something very strange indeed skimming the surface. Considered too big to be an aircraft, America spent the next twenty years wondering what the hell it was.

And what was it? breathed Bo, shivering with excitement.

The KM Ekranoplan.

Dewei was laughing so much he could hardly contain himself.

The Soviets were testing the world's heaviest flying machine, except it was not an aircraft.

Then what was it?

A monster.

To which everyone except Bo whee-wheed and whoo-whooed

with amusement; she simply felt betrayed to be made to appear so foolish. And it hurt.

Oh look, called Lok, who had already spotted a rare creature. Big fish!

Sturgeon, identified Chung. Very valuable to humans.

Want or need?

Want, replied Chung. It's being fished to death. Take a good look and show respect, because one day they will all be gone.

Will we all be gone one day? asked Hu-tu anxiously.

We will be gone, of course, but if we work hard enough to ensure our survival, our children and grandchildren will follow on.

Let's just hope humans never change their minds and decide they like the taste of us, Lok noted with feeling. And for the first time thought about all the creatures that he ate with such relish, without any consideration for their own future survival.

Why don't ducks tell jokes when they're flying? he asked as they gathered concentration for take off. It was so much easier to amuse than have to think too seriously.

Because they would quack up, eight replied in unison. They knew Lok's sense of humour better than he knew it himself.

By this time, of course, they were all far more conscious of one another's strengths and weaknesses than they were able to acknowledge and admit their own. Though they had begun ...

Turkmenistan

It was in China, late one moonless night
The Simurgh first appeared in mortal sight –
He let a feather float down through the air
And rumours of its fame spread everywhere.
Farid Al-Din Attar (The Conference of Birds)

The port of Baku was soon left behind, and the Turkmenistan coast drew them forward with overiding scents on the wind of water and desert and ancient memories of migration.

This place was on our Water Road, linking east and west, recalled Chung, delighted. He was even more thrilled when clever Cong led them south of Krasnovodsk to where Turkmenbashi Bay offered a surprisingly welcome safe haven from all the refineries, ship repair yards and food processing factories of the city.

What an amazing place, breathed Hu-tu and Bo in unison, so ruffling their plumage in such astonishment that they loosened one prettily pale feather here, and another there ... For on every side – shallow brackish bays, spits, islands and dunes – were water birds of every size and colour and shape imaginable, most of which they had never seen before in their lives.

As for Chung, he was near speechless. But, being Chung, of course he was not.

Down south, on the northern coast of Iran is a city called Ramsar, he explained. That is where some thoughtful humans gathered years ago to confer, talk about our future and finds ways to protect us. Now there are over two hundred salt and freshwater wetlands conserved all over the world, and Cong, Dewei, Shuang, Hu-tu and Bo, you might like to know that the largest number are in Britain, where you began your journey.

Maybe we could call a conference to establish whether there are any Mandarins around here who might like to come along, suggested Dewei. I know this is not our normal habitat, but you never know ...

Good idea, agreed Chung and Chii-Nii.

And look, pointed Shuang, flapping his wings with excitement. For more and more birds were arriving from the north, swooshing down all around as far as the eye could see.

The reason was quickly made clear. As a stopover and wintering port of call, the bay site encompassed two important migratory routes, the Afro-Eurasian Flyway and part of the Central Asian-Indian Flyway.

If you can get your brains around the numbers, said Chung, some five to eight million water birds pass along this coast on migration, and up to eight hundred thousand winter right here. So some of those you see landing may stay, but most will rest and take advantage of the rich feeding ground and then head further south.

Wow, breathed Lok, caught up for once in the interest of facts rather than the promise of food. Still, doesn't that make us rather odd, because we are going east?

Yes, agreed Chung. We are very odd indeed. But most of these birds nest in Western Siberia, Kazakhstan and other regions of Northern Asia. So we are all a long way from home.

Let's fly around a bit, suggested Shuang: put out the word, ask if there are any Mandarins, or if any are expected. As you say,

Chung, this is not our native habitat, but as Deiwei voiced, you never know.

There was no need to move far, because the word spread fast, and soon Mandarin ducks were heading their way from up and down the coast and way inland. A pair here, a cluster there, several singles and finally a ragged group of thirty, all of whom claimed to be following a feather.

NEWS TRAVELS IN MANY WAYS

A feather?

It seems that three feathers – blue, black, green – had been fluttering and floating all over Europe and beyond, spreading news of an epic journey to China. All the newcomers had heard of them, had followed them on water, on the wind, and via the networking of forests and woodland, while all the time staying in tune with universal energies ...

Soon they were gathered, with Chii-nii working overtime interpreting any number of languages – even Russian! Other water birds began to show interest, wondering what all the excitement was about, as some fifty Mandarins whoo-whooed with expectation before the Group of Nine and the secondary group ranged behind.

Something was happening, something was happening ... but what?

Order, order! commanded Dewei, rather pompously, the others thought.

Order, order? echoed Shuang, hooting with amusement. Come off it. Remember who and what we are.

Chung moved forward and quietly began to explain who and what they were: Mandarin ducks, heading for their ancestral home.

It was a new concept to most of those water birds gathered, the large majority of whom had never heard of Mandarins before, let alone seen one.

What about us? queried an endangered White-Headed duck. Are we welcome to come along to ensure the survival of our species?

Chii-nii looked sad. They could assure nothing, she advised. Humans believe everything on earth is their own for the taking. Not even humans are safe from humans. Why, even those abusers who are hurting and killing one another and destroying their own home, Mother Earth, are too unconscious to realize the folly of their ways.

Agreement rippled around the congregation. Birds did not dirty their own nests. They respected their own kind. And yet …

We Mandarins are too small and fragile to survive, Chii-nii continued. We have nothing humans want. It would be good to think they need us to help keep nature in balance, but most humans are not even aware that without nature in balance we are all doomed.

The crowd fell silent. But not for too long.

I'd just like to come along and keep you all company, indicated a sociable Lapwing. We are critically endangered, you know, and need all the advice and encouragement we can get. I have to say, you do seem very organised, exceptionally strong and focussed.

The Nine looked from one to the other, with Chii-nii taking the lead.

We each have our own journey, she noted. For those of you struggling to survive human development, which in so many ways is more destructive that constructive, I think you'd be wise to stay and follow your natural instincts. Fly the routes your ancestors have flown since time immemorial and have faith that conscious humans continue to create safe havens like this until there are linked routes all around the world and we can move around freely in health and safety. It is different for us; we are simply exiles trying to find our way home. We wish you luck, though.

The others all nodded in agreement. Which set what they had named The New Nine behind them nodding in unison, so that soon there were eighteen little heads bobbing gravely up and down.

So who likes to gamble? Lok said, changing the mood. Who would like to come along? Who'll fly with us to China?

Some Mandarins said, yes and others said no, and the large majority wavered in-between.

The conference continued well into the evening, when together all the birds, irrespective of species, language, gender or creed, collectively faced and bowed to the setting sun. Giving thanks for the day, they watched it sink prettily into a pearly pink sea.

FROM FEAST TO FAMINE

Some seventy birds left the next morning, which, while pleasing Chii-nii and Chung, rather shocked the others. They never imagined that what had begun as a dream could be transforming into such an odyssey.

Their shock increased as they left such watery vistas behind and were soon flying over sand dunes that gave way to scrubby undulating – and unrelenting – desert.

It was over one especially hot spot that in near shock Chung shed a small cloud of dramatically colourful feathers, including purple, red, yellow and gold, allowing them to fall onto the wasteland below.

They flew close but in several groups, and always with Cong and the others in the lead. He followed the route of the Karakum Canal for a fresh water and food supply, which crossed the country irrigating much of the land for cotton. But the canal was a mess, leaking into ponds and rivulets that drew salt from the old seabed of the desert land and in danger of making things worse rather than better.

It was not all bad news, of course. There were villages and farms, and local people shouted with pleasure when the ducks flew overhead.

Hey, welcome, called an older man working in a cotton field. Water is a Turkmen's life …

Welcome, welcome, yelled a young man racing through scrub land near a stud farm from the back of an Akhal-Teke, an ancient breed of golden horse that shimmers and gleams like polished metal. A horse is his wings …

Welcome winged ones, greeted a student of philosophy. Did you know that in Arabic our hieroglyphic writing is called the language of birds?

Welcome and safe journey, sang a woman weaving up a tree of life in a landscape where trees were the subject of myth and everyone prayed five times a day, their heads pointing towards Mecca. A carpet is His – and my – soul …

Such rare riches apart, it was a relief to cross the border. But then things got worse.

Afghanistan

Why do birds sing in the morning? It's the triumphant shout: "We got through another night!"

Enid Bagnold

As far as Mazari-Sharif the terrain was not so different. But then mountains reared up and never before had the convoy seen or experienced such cruel terrain.

Cruel things have happened here and all over the rest of this country, said Chung. And witnessing Hu-tu and Bo in sisterly solidarity dropping more soft feathers, breathed sighs of relief to see where they fell: on jagged crags and in rocky ravines, over rocks and earth and every geological formation imaginable where nothing in living memory had ever grown.

Surviving in such treacherous landscapes was hard to imagine, they thought collectively as they flew over dusty streets, equally dusty patches of scrub and trees, flat-topped rooftops strung with washing and the famed blue-tiled shrine of Hazrat Ali.

Then came an airport, but one so strangely active that it was hard to equate with airports they had already seen. For one thing, there were so many planes and helicopters and trucks and loaders and pieces of such large-scale machinery that it was hard to imagine what they were used for. While inbetween, every inch of ground was moving, squirming, seemingly alive.

They are military personnel wearing camouflage, uniforms made from fabric printed in the same colours as the earth, so that they cannot be seen by enemies, observed Chung as they alighted at dusk at the eastern end of the airport, outside the perimeter fence.

Some job, grunted Cong cynically, not at all impressed.

What's an enemy? asked Bo.

Someone you want to kill.

Why?

Because you hate them, for what they have or what they want, or what they stand for. Or it's their work.

Sounds silly to me, she murmered to no-one in particular. I mean, I get annoyed, but it never goes any further than that, because I am always watching my irritation, observing myself in action and realising both the foolishness of my behaviour and my reaction to it.

Chii-nii gazed at Bo in surprise and admiration. For a small duck she had come a very long way in so short a time, and Chii-nii was not thinking about how far she had flown.

Why so much activity here, though,? wondered Shuang. And the noise! for the landscape echoed with the sounds of gunfire and explosions.

In reply, all agog, they heard Chung talk of Russia and America, and how now various countries were involved in trying to free the population – especially the women – from suppressive forces of masculine tribal values. But was not having foreign soldiers all over the place, the sky rattling with the sound of heavy metal and the earth being beaten and blown up also suppressive? It was all very complicated.

And none of our business, concluded Dewei. Where to from here? The Hindu Kush? Oh my, do we have to? I wish the next twenty-four hours were over. What a harsh and cruel country this is.

Harsh and beautiful, continued Li Qin, who, being all for creating a bit of additional excitement in her life, found the thought of seemingly endless rugged mountain ranges hugely exhilarating in their challenge.

But mostly harsh and dangerous, feared Lok, who was remembering the safe comfort of the gentle waters of the Danube and the relaxed languid summer with a deep nostalgia.

BETTER SAFE THAN SORRY

To say it was a relief to drop down into the Panjshir Valley towards the Shamali Plains is an understatement. The city of Charikar seemed quiet enough, with only the turning of potters' wheels and the stamping of feet on late pickings of grapes disturbing the air. But Chung warned they ought not to linger.

There was an attack right in the heart of the town just last year, he recalled. The usual suspects claimed responsibility.

Let's move on, he urged. I know you are all tired, but Jalalabad is not far, and then it's on through the Khyber Pass into Pakistan. We can wait there a day or so for any stragglers to catch up and regain our energy.

It was true. They were in Jalalabad within the day. Maybe flying downhill helped, noted Lok, ever the joker.

NOTHING IS AS IT SEEMS

Finding so much fresh water in the city, situated as it is where two rivers converge, the Kabul and the Kunar, proved akin to landing in paradise.

After so many days of heavy concentrated effort, it was wonderful just to bathe and soak and let their muscles unwind.

I have heard that at the right time of the year, the gardens are full of orange blossom, mused Hu-tu. How blissful that must be.

I have heard that also in early summer, the land around here, called Nangarhar Province, is ablaze with poppies, recalled Lok. What a wonderful sight that must be.

I have heard that making opium from their seed heads is illegal and does incredible harm to already damaged human beings, noted Chung. As for the colour, seen from high above where we fly, it surely mirrors all the human blood spilled over the centuries.

This place has been the centre of philosophical and religious struggles between Buddhists, Muslims, Hindus and those adhering to local beliefs and superstitions since the Dark Ages, he continued sadly.

Dear friends, interrupted Chii-nii gently but firmly. It is not for us to resolve human problems. Though if they were to watch our progress and take our advice, they might learn much to their advantage.

And so saying, she fell asleep and began weaving a dream about reaching their final destination and finding the world ready and willing to wake up.

She looked very lovely in her sleeping state, thought Cong, wondering why she was smiling.

Pakistan

Be like the bird in flight ... pausing a while on boughs too slight, feels them give way beneath her, yet sings knowing yet, that she has wings.

Victor Marie Hugo

To fly right into the heart of a city and find the perfect place to hang out was a surprise to everyone.

Rawal Lake Park in the centre of Islamabad was scattered with small wooded islands that provided the Mandarins with a habitat that made them feel instantly at home. They could perch, they could swim, they could walk, and in perfect safety.

This has to be China, said Bo, not for the first time wanting to stay put having arrived somewhere comfortable. Please tell me this is China.

Sorry but no, Chung said, patting her head. This is Pakistan, which used to be part of India, but chose to break away and create its own country.

Why did they do that?

Because of religion. Pakistan is a Muslim country, and India largely follows the Hindu faith.

The boughs of the tree in which he was sitting were so over-crowded with Mandarins that branches were bending low, in some cases almost touching the ground.

I don't understand all these isms that you have been talking about since we first met, said Shuang. Socialism, Communism, Fascism, Catholicism, Hinduism, Jainism ... And then there are all these other ... what do you call them, religions ... Christianity, Islam, Judaism, Buddhism ... Why is human life all so complicated, making the life of the rest of the world so complicated?

Because the human brain is a complex organ.

Do we have brains?

Sometimes I wonder, joked Chung, nudging Bo so that she almost fell off the branch.

As I understand it, continued Cong from where Chung had left off, the human brain has two lobes, and the right-hand one handles perception and creativity, while the left is concerned with logic and thinking.

Chii-nii looked at him sideways with a new respect. This young male also learns fast, she thought.

I guess that makes me more left-brain than right, rationalised Dewei.

And I am as right-brain as they come, intuited Chii-nii. Sometimes I think I could do with a bit of your left brain …

As I could do with a degree of your own lovely lobe, agreed Dewei in the most charming manner he could come up with, while at the same time wondering on the quiet if the ducklings they created might not be the most perfectly balanced ducks ever born.

Not so simple, corrected Chii-nii, who of course knew what he was thinking. We need a ninth of all our individual strengths to make ourselves whole, become the best we can possibly be in any situation.

But not our weaknesses, agreed Dewei, so embarrassed that if he had been human he would have blushed.

Absolutely, piped up Hu-tu. Though she was not at all sure what her own weaknesses were … if she had any, of course, believing herself to be a martyr to the cause, any cause.

Chung hated to pull them away from where they were obviously so happy and relaxed, but it had to be done, and done quickly before they all became just too comfortable.

The next stretch would be long but immeasurably interesting, he explained to the gathered assembly next morning.

Try not to get too involved in what is going on below, which will be filled with curiosity and stories, music and song, together with endless vistas of natural beauty, but keep your eyes on the path ahead.

We will be flying across the Punjab – which many believe is where the Roma originated – south of the Himalayas, to avoid Tibet. Not because it would not be an amazing experience to visit such a brave and strongly independent country, but I fear it really would be just too physically hard for us.

So, India, Nepal, Myanmar, he listed on one foot, and then on into China … (on the other)

Well, they all agreed, whoo-whooing with excitement, that didn't sound so bad. And began revving up for lift off.

India

Leg-spinning cricket champion B. S. Chandrasekhar had minimal batting skills ... He was given a special Gray-Nicolls bat during the 1977-78 Australian tour with a hole in it to commemorate the four ducks he scored. He has 23 ducks to his credit.

Wikipedia

Though he tried hard to live up to his own advice, it was difficult for Chung not to send word that they were passing over Amritsar as the spiritual centre of the Sikh religion.

Shuang groaned. Not another religion!

Also, Chung continued, it was where the British army shot one thousand Indian people – men, women and children – in the public garden.

Hu-tu was horrified. Why would people from the country where she had been born do such a terrible thing?

They were scared, Cong explained. They reacted out of fear that they were losing control of the country they'd claimed as their own. And they were right. That event proved to be the beginning of the end of the British Empire.

But there was a tangible legacy ... in the infrastructure – especially the trains that the ducks saw criss-crossing the land they passed over ... in the games children played in the streets ... in the sing-song English they heard on occasion.

India also had its own legacy, Chung reminded them, never better expressed than by Bengal's most famous poet, Rabindranath Tagore. And naturally enough, Chung being Chung, he could recall whole chunks of verse.

My favourite line? Faith is the bird that feels the light and sings when the dawn is still dark.

Soon after they flew over the Sutlej, flowing down from the mountains of Kashmir where it sourced. It would go on and join the Chenab, from Pakistan, to become the mighty Indus that emerges into the Arabian Sea south of Karachi.

Still in the grip of the monsoon season, with the landscape green and watery, the route was refreshing and beautiful, but they did not stop other than to briefly drink and nap.

Then it was on to Ambala, and after another hundred miles or so, Roorkee, a small town on the banks of the Ganges Canal, and the home of one of the largest technical institutes in Asia.

Pity we missed Cognizance, the huge festival they hold every spring, noted Chung. We'd have learned a lot about technological advances; for all their mistakes humans are very clever and may save themselves yet! But then remembering his vocation added, Not that it's anything to do with us.

Having crossed into the lower lands of Uttar Pradesh, Pilibhit offered distractions well suited to survival, being flat and liquid and covered in forest. Li Qin was especially entranced to hear that the region was also known as Bansuri Nagari, meaning Land of the Flutes, and made a brief detour with Hu-tu and Bo to find a family on the outskirts that helped supply India with the large majority of such instruments .

Hu-tu returned, horrified. Dear, dear, she kept repeating.

The people are so poor, she explained. No kitchen, just a few pots. No bathroom at all. Just the stream, for everything!

They would be Dalit in the Indian caste system, Chung said. Untouchables.

Untouchables? None of the Mandarins could understand such a concept. They were all equal, were they not? And touched wingtips to answer the question, make the point.

But are we equal to swans and grebes, storks, pigeons and parrots? queried Dewei.

Of course! they all replied, putting him firmly in his place.

Ideals are fine, he muttered, but what if some birds don't see it the same way.

Some of the newly joined Mandarins murmered in agreement, thinking Dewei had a point.

Oh dear, thought Chung and Chii-nii, hoping Dewei would relent and not cause dissent among the ranks.

Dewei was still trying to recover reason when they took off in yet another driving gust of life-giving rain for Nepalgunj, just over the border.

Nepal

Retreat the birds who are wandering around without a purpose...

Bikash Vital

God, why are we here? It's a nice enough small town but so hot, moaned Bo. Hot and so humid.

Good point, agreed Shuang, who was at this point in the lead. We'll try to take an easier breath around Birgunj.

But this larger municipality proved even more heated, being the gateway between Nepal and India and as busy as busy can be.

And so they came to Biratnagar, meaning in Nepali, Huge City, and so it was, by comparison with others passed over at least. Luckily the soil around was fertile, and so they were able to rest awhile beside a small house where a woman with a third eye (and wearing a yellow sari) was kind enough to allow them temporary landing rights.

A widow, the woman with a third eye lived with her children who were away at school or working. She herself earned a meagre living by twisting strands of jute together to make ropes for a local speciality of the Dashain festival: linge pings, swings made of three bamboo poles tied together.

Li Qin tried a sample and thought it great fun, a marvellous opportunity to show off a few acrobatics.

All was well until the woman's family began to drift home and then things got altogether too noisy and intrusive; instead the flock moved on to a farm where a green herb was being cultivated and they could paddle and feed in muddy irrigation ditches.

It was Lok, of course, who first thought to taste the unfamiliar plant: Stevia rebaudiana. And what a surprise!

The leaves are sweet, he exclaimed. Really sweet. As sweet as the wetlands were salty, remember?

They did. What a long time ago that seemed already. Another world.

We must get a move on, urged Cong.

Indeed, agreed Chung. But first I crave your patience. For there is a small detour we need to make.

Oh no, groaned Dewei and Shuang, remembering York. Not another.

Indeed there were rumblings of discontent on all sides, with several of the newcomers beginning to question the whole purpose of the trip. Might it not be better to go back?

But this time, it was not Chung but Chii-nii who put on the pressure. She had a feeling, she said. She had a powerful intuition that they just had to sidetrack to Darjeeling.

India (again)

He was so benevolent, so merciful a man that, in his mistaken passion, he would have held an umbrella over a duck in a shower of rain.

Douglas Jerrold

Not so far eastwards, they were back in India again, the whirlwind but fast-exhausting monsoon still whipping their tails. The creation of Bangladesh had resulted in a narrow corridor of Indian territory to the north, opening out into Assam.

There was so much distraction: the hill stations; steep rolling slopes covered with tea bushes; the colourful saris of women at work; the huffing-puffing of a mountain steam train that snaked ever upwards ...

But Chung retained his focus, leading them directly to the north, up and up along the border with Nepal to West Bengal and Darjeeling. Here he landed in a tea plantation called Makaibari that he described as premium organic, bio-dynamic. He and Chii-nii seemed very excited by this, even if the others were clueless

We have passed over so many hillsides and terraces of tea plantations, she said, as the others landed, bouncing between the lines of sparkling tea bushes (it had just rained) on the softest, most friable soil imaginable. But this is the first where crops were planted and harvested according to natural bio-rythmns and prescribed rituals.

And with no artificially designed chemicals to boost production and limit bugs and disease, added Chung. Everything lives in harmony. Even the tigers pass through in peace and safety, offering no danger to man or beast.

Tigers? queried Bo.

Big stripey cats that can turn into man-eaters if under attack.

Bo was not fond of cats. Or – remembering the beast from long ago that had all but torn her wing off – dogs. But she liked the sound of harmony. She'd always been big on harmony.

Dewei was peeved again. Actually he was more than peeved. He was seething.

Do you mean we have come this extra distance just to sit in dirt?

No, we came to see history in the making. This is the oldest commercial tea plantation in the region, and the first to believe in the interaction between soil, plants and animals as a holistic self-sustaining system. Its fourth-generation owner was considered crazy when he began farming in this way. Nowadays, while technically retired, he is much respected and admired ... and all because he had a dream.

Li Qin – already light-headed due to the altitude – perked up considerably when she heard this. Maybe that was what she needed in order to become a star: a dream. She immediately went to sleep for a quick nap, completely misunderstanding that the dream Chung was talking about was nothing to do with being unconscious, but quite the opposite.

When she woke soon after, not a single duck noticed her slip away. Slip away to try her luck on the silver screen. Not even Lok.

He was with the others, grubbing about in a stream finding delicious morsels of this and that, quite oblivious to the grumpy mutterings of wanting to – needing to – move on. It was only later that he realised Li Qin was nowhere to be seen, and set off – quite an arduous journey in its own right – to track her down.

In the meantime Cong, Shuang and Hu-tu were curious. They wanted to know more about bio-dynamic farming.

So they learned about Silver Tips Imperial, picked under a full moon and recorded as the world's most expensive tea.

And then – even more exciting because of being so personal – they heard of a tea created by ancient Chinese tea masters called Bai Mu Dan, or White Tea which, promising eternal youth, appealed to the extreme vanity and deep pockets of ancient bureaucratic Mandarins no less!

Also that before this plantation in Kurseong, meaning White Orchid, was founded many years ago now, only Chinese and Japanese specialists practised the craft or art, depending on your point of view, of growing and making tea.

Was it coincidental or synchronistic that within the hour, a lone Mandarin flew down from the northwest and alighted on a tea bush, causing consternation all around?

The main reason for the surprised concern was clear for all to see.

He was white.

NO ACCIDENTAL TOURIST

Even Chung, who was rarely surprised by anything, found himself voiceless. He had never seen or heard of such a phenomena: a pure white Mandarin.

Sometimes females were paler than the rest, but this male was as white as snow – as white as the peaks of the Himalayas that continued to keep pace, rising like an endless wall of jagged teeth to the left as they flew along the base of the foothills. Now of course they lay directly ahead, from where the ghost-like white bird had manifested.

Whispers travelled at the speed of light around the group.

Was he real? Had he fallen into a pot of milk or whitewash? Was he some other kind of bird masquerading as a Mandarin just to get to China? Was he an abominable snowbird? Was he a god, flown from the top of Mt Everest – just as the goddess Chii-nii had flown down from the top of a windmill – appearing as one of their own so as not to cause alarm?

Chii-nii was thinking along the same lines herself, when a far more alarming thought came to mind.

Where are you from? she asked gently.

The white Mandarin replied so faintly few could hear. Also he communicated in a language even fewer could understand.

He is from Russia, Chii-nii announced softly. From a place called Chernobyl.

Chung made a small sound in his throat that meant nothing to any of them.

The name Chernobyl meant nothing to the congregation either, except Chii-nii and Chung.

There was an accident there several generations ago, the goddess explained, the worst known accident in his and her-story. Now the air, the water and the land all around are poisoned for years to come. Most of the humans living and working roundabout ran away to escape the terrible effects on their bodies, and the bodies of their children, and their children's children.

This Mandarin's ancestors were only passing through when the accident occurred; they stayed because afterwards they felt weak and then when people moved away, they had the countryside to themselves. More than this he does not know, except that several of his brothers and sisters were born with deformities and he was born white.

Deformities? echoed Hu-tu, hesitantly, not knowing what this new word meant.

Strange-shaped heads. Only one wing. Twisted feet. No eyes …

A shudder of horror ran through the assembly. One or two began to cry. Several backed away, as if fearful of contagion.

What caused such a horrible thing to happen? wondered Dewei.

Humans playing with the basic structure of the universe – atoms, particles, energy, vibration – over which ultimately they have no control, contributed Chung, who had by now largely recovered himself.

It was beyond his comprehension that anyone could believe in one hundred per cent safety, believe their actions infallible, when messing around with things that were beyond understanding. There is no such thing ... always room for error, for natural or unnatural intervention, for the unexpected, unplanned, unconsidered, unimagined.

How did he know we were here? asked Bo, who thought this latest arrival the most exotic creature she had ever come across in her life.

One day a small blue feather had floated past on the stream where he'd been living since early summer. It carried a message: fly southeast, join the Nine in One. Curious, he decided to make the trip. Though he never expected to fly so long or so high ... or to do so quite so successfully.

He says he may be a mutant, but he is an exceptionally strong and resilient mutant.

Chii-niii stopped to take breath. Translating through a waterfall of compassionate tears was far from easy. Were there any Mandarins from Russia in the new group with duckepathic abilities? she called ... to give herself a break, time to dry her eyes and re-settle her plumage.

Honestly, she confided to Chung. The sooner we all speak one language the better.

Like we used to, before we became split and separate, seeking individuality, wanting to be different, he agreed.

How about I work on a form of Ducksperanto? she suggested:

a language common to us all. This would help us bond while developing our duckepathic skills. Our group of one is doing well, and the new group of nine is showing interest as well as talent. As for the rest, time will tell ...

And so it was decided. And the white duck was designated a talisman, a good luck charm for the future. A symbol of Mandarin duck – any kind of duck, or bird for that matter – over adversity. Which, while not eliciting any direct response, seemed to please him very much.

Chung also gave him a name, Fai, meaning beginning, or a brilliant light. He had considered the obvious, Bai, for white, but that was too simple; he wanted a name that conveyed this duck's unique status, his as yet unrevealed role in their journey, and his value – if any – in evolution of the species.

Naturally enough, Fai's sudden elevation led to great complaint among the unsettled rest, especially among the nine who had joined in Hungary, because they all wanted to be named too. The widowed female, who was especially outspoken in her desire for identification, had already begun calling herself Xiao Chen for early morning, signifying a new start.

Chung and Chii-nii were still racking their bird brains well past midnight, trying to come up with appellations that seemed appropriate. Since they knew little to nothing about any of the Mandarins who had joined in Turkmenistan, they had to rely on relatives, friends and casual observers for advice. And this was taxing their patience and energy reserves to the limit.

I wish we had not started this, Chung grumbled, in dire need of his beauty sleep.

To which Chii-nii replied with a quick but careful spell that put all the recent comers to sleep in a jiffy, and during which they all forgot about names. It was not the most enlightened of moves, but it certainly helped in the short term.

What a relief to wake in the morning and find everything

back to normal! Even one white duck that no one thought at all unusual; rather with newly open minds they regarded Fai without anger, fear or envy.

HAPPY LAND

The next day they spent flying along the border with Bhutan, reputed to be the happiest country in the world because the King and his people were in agreement to keep Western-style development and its many excesses and distractions at bay.

Bo wanted to go and take a look, and indeed it was a tempting idea. But the flying was easy, the weather kind, they were never far from water, and China was calling.

China may be calling you, Chung, but Bhutan is calling me, Bo claimed. She could feel its vibration, and it was good. China? She was not so sure.

I have heard things, she added. And they are not all encouraging.

Well, I doubt anywhere is perfect, interjected Chii-nii. Only Shangri-la is, and that is in our imagination – the sum of past life recall.

I thought Makaibari was a pretty perfect happy place, Shuang broke in, wishing they could have stayed longer, if not forever. The air felt fresh. Streams ran clear. The land was happy. Tea bushes were happy. Everything that lived there claimed to be happy. And I think I have never seen a happier man than the protector of tigers, waving us off from under his umbrella.

The man with a dream; the man making his dream come true.

Which was just what Li Qin had tried to do back in the city of Darjeeling, make her own dream come true: by creeping away with the idea to audition for a Bollywood movie.

Fortunately once again she was saved from her egoic self. Because if Lok had not woken to her absence, followed her trail and been able to tear her away before she made a fool of herself prancing in front of the cameras, nine would have reduced to seven, and all their stories would have taken a very different turn.

I don't know, said Dewei, pointing a wing feather accusingly at Li Qin without realizing he was pointing three at himself. We fly for hundreds of miles without incident, and then without warning or for any particular reason, suddenly everything goes haywire.

That is the chaos theory, pronounced Chung. There are only two things we can expect to be sure of in life: death, and the unexpected. Now there's an irony!

In the meantime, he said loudly so that the whole convoy could hear, let us appreciate what we have in this moment.

Happiness, they all chorused in Ducksperanto. For Chii-nii had taken advantage of the stopover to complete her dictionary and upload it en masse for instant access.

Chung was delighted, for Chii-nii had done nothing less than revive the ancient common language of birds, considered by the Kabbalah and Renaissance magic and alchemy to be not only a secret and perfect language, but also the key to perfect knowledge. It was so attuned with nature at its most balanced, he elaborated, that sometimes it was called the *langue verte* or green language.

Chii-nii looked abashed. She had known this, of course. And something more: that in Sufism - yes, another ism, she apologised – the language of birds was the mystical language of angels.

The common language of the birds rippled around the gathered throng.

Now they could all communicate. Not only were they a community. They were an angelic host.

BLOOD THICKER THAN WATER

There were many fast-flowing rivers joining the Brahmaputra in and around the town of Tezpur. In turn it swelled the Ganges Delta to empty into the Bay of Bengal, a journey of two thousand nine hundred kilometres from source: the snow and ice melt of Himalayan glaciers.

Named from words in Sanskrit that meant blood and town or city, in reference to its bloody history, most inhabitants of Tezpur preferred to point visitors to an inscription on the Kaliyabhomora Bridge: Welcome to the City of Love.

Love, sighed Hu-tu. Will I ever find it? Will it ever find me?

Love, sighed Lok and Li Qin, all forgiven and once again in complete harmony.

Love, sighed Bo. Sometimes it hurts.

Love, sighed Cong. Bring it on!

Love, sighed Dewei, wondering if it might mess up his routine.

Love, sighed Shuang. I think it may be the answer to everything.

Love, sighed Chung, directing a personalised tail feather swift as an arrow into the aether to reach the soul of his mate and tell her he was on his way. A manymanymany-splendoured thing …

Myanmar

Even within the tropics, a land where migration would seem unnecessary, birds move with the seasonal rains and droughts across hundreds of miles, following the blossoming of flowers, the ripening of fruit.

Scott Weidensaul (Living on the Wind: Across the Hemisphere with Migratory Birds)

The stretch across the northern triangular of tip of Myanmar offered only one significant landmark of human habitation after crossing the border from India: Putao, the City of Gold.

For the ducks, such wealth had to be in the clean air, fresh water and magnificent views to the north of the mountains, including the peak known as Hkakabo Razi, rising to nearly six thousand metres as if to celebrate the handshake of India, Myamnar and China.

Being sub-tropical it was hotter and more humid than ever before; with uncharted wooded rocky valleys secreted with rare orchids and an abundance of endemic wildlife in an eco-system that remained intact and unsullied, it was a place of indescribable beauty.

Humans come here only in summer, explained Chung. In winter it is locked away, impenetrable.

The ducks were lying crumpled and exhausted on the side of a valley, while in the surrounding terraced paddy fields tribal men and women worked shoulder to shoulder cutting rice by hand and singing to maintain their spirit and rhythm.

Harvest is later here because we're so much higher, noted Chung.

All this going up and down is so distracting, complained Bo. I like to know where I am: up or down.

Yes, and think how much time we'd save if we didn't need to keep resting all the time, added Dewei.

But think hard about whether you would like to be a Sooty tern, that leaves its nest and then stays airborne for three to ten years, noted Chung.

What? Never landing at all? Bo's feathers were nearly standing on end at the mere thought.

Occasionally it settles on water. And of course it has to land to breed.

Well, yes, I was wondering about that, Hu-tu replied with a gasp of relief.

How far can we migrate? wondered Cong. I mean, we know we have got this far, but just how strong are we?

I do know that a Common tern banded by ornithologists in Finland, to the far north, was found perfectly healthy in southern Australia seven months later. That is over sixteen thousand miles, so it must have flown over a hundred and twenty-five miles a day.

Chii-nii was settled near Fai, picking up on his thoughts.

He believes he could fly forever without stopping, she relayed to the others. He thinks he may be more than a mutant. He wonders if he is a completely new species of bird, with powers beyond all understanding. Why, humans are only just beginning to understand that we birds are guided by a magnetic compass which enables us to detect magnetic fields via chemical reactions inside individual cells in our bodies.

Wow, breathed Shuang, deeply impressed. Is that true?

There are many things humans do not understand about us – meaning birds in general, replied Chung. The tragedy is that as their knowledge increases, our numbers decrease. Our brilliance will be recorded – but sadly we will be gone.

How else are we brilliant? asked Bo.

We have a nictating membrane, a transluscent third eyelid that acts to protect our eyes while retaining perfect vision, when flying for example. Nictating? It means to blink. Humans have lost their own, with only a tiny nub in the inner corner of their eyes remaining.

Also some birds can smell an earthworm through inches of soil.

Useful, admired Lok.

But migration patterns really have humans wondering. Because we Mandarins were bred domestically, our migratory instinct is not strong. But when many birds are caged, they often hop about and get very frustrated when they are supposed to start migrating in the wild. They know. They just know …

We are brilliant! crowed Bo and Hu-tu in unison.

Chung, Dewei and Shuang joined in, and then all the other Mandarins began to voice too: they were as one: brilliant.

Most brilliant of all, Fai began to glow luminously, as if lit from within.

SO CLOSE

Not far now, encouraged Chung. Really, we are so close to the border.

Will we know? asked Cong, whose internal compass indicated magnetic direction but not artificially introduced lines on a map.

I will voice, confirmed Chung. And then we will celebrate.

Celebrate with what? How? wondered Li Qin.

If we were in France, we could open a bottle of Mandarine Napoleon Brandy. But since we will be in our own homeland, and alcohol is an anathema for ducks set on flying in a straight line, maybe a nip of fresh Chinese water will have to do.

China

If I keep a green bough in my heart, then the singing bird will come.
Chinese proverb

It was only when they crossed the mightily muddy Mekong River that flowed to the south through Yunnan Province that it really sank in: they were in China.

Do you realize we have crossed some of the largest and most important rivers in the world? Chung reflected, gazing out over yet another powerful waterway. All of them flowing to the south from the Himalayas. The question is, of course, what will happen when the glaciers retreat and snowfall reduces to the point that fresh water is at a premium?

We will be thirsty, observed Lok drily.

We will be stuck? queried Bo.

Life will be stuck, Chung answered. Nature will have to adapt or die.

Jolly! sniped Dewei, fed up with bad news. Can we consider something more positive, or not talk at all? I mean, look at Fai. It's so restful to fly with a duck who chooses stillness over acrobatics and silence over mindless chatter.

It was true. Even when not in flight, Fai remained still and soundless, choosing not to speak. He had not consciously taken a vow of silence, rather had nothing to say ... There were no words. Instead he found comfort in silence. His own silence.

What can I say about what happened to me? he thought. I could be sad. I could be angry. I could be resentful. Instead I choose to be none of these things because they are meaningless. I simply accept. I exist in the moment, without judgment, without revenge, without fear. I am what I am, for better, for worse.

Bo wondered if this deep and mysterious duck might mate, if he was interested in having a family. But no sooner had the thought entered her mind than Fai was responding ... No, he was infertile, he could not procreate.

Sad, she thought, hugely disappointed. But what about sex? Might he be interested in making love if not hatchlings?

Again, no. He had no sex drive either. He was nothing, he said, dry-eyed but his heart cracking with a repressed emotion that existed in a vacuum, as did he.

I am like a eunuch, he thought. Sexless. Worthless. What is the point of my making this journey, even being alive?

With the speed of light, Chii-nii wove a net of love around him to hold him tight.

Don't think like that, she relayed. You are here for a reason, just as we are all here for a reason. You have a mission. It is simply not clear yet what this mission is. Have faith as before, when you left Chernobyl. You jumped and see? the net catches you every time.

Fai stilled his fears once more, remembering what his grandfather had taught him long ago: the past is history, tomorrow is a mystery, today is a gift and that was why it is called the present.

It is true, he thought before stilling mind, body and spirit once more, his heartbeat slowing and temperature dropping: there is only the present moment, and that is why it is so treasured.

A CHINESE POND IN A CHINESE PARK

It was not often that Chung got things wrong, but on the subject of alcohol, he was way out.

There was enormous excitement as the ducks descended onto the flat plateau that gave the town – virtually untouched and unaltered for over eight hundred years – its name: Dayan, or the big Ink Stone. They really were in China.

Questions flew thick and fast.

The Nine in One knew what Chinese people looked like after their summer in Budapest, but most of the others did not so they wondered, would the natives be friendly? How far did they have to go now, and why fly another inch if this place proved to be as picture perfect as first appearances suggested?

It was Lok who decided to take a posse into town. To check it out, he said. Cong intimated he would like to go too: to keep an eye on things (meaning Lok). Shuang was simply keen to be with his brothers and join the others, for several young male newcomers had clamoured to be taken along.

Chung decided to stay put on Black Dragon pool in Jade Spring Park just to the north of the city of Lijiang, of which Dayan was one half. Fringed with willows, the tasty green water was as clear as clear can be, with a waterfall, a Moon Embracing Pavilion linked to a marble bridge, and a Five Phoenix Pagoda. Really, could a Chinese duck want for more?

While tired to the bone, Chung knew how far they still had to go. In many ways this last stretch would be the toughest, but such was the uncontrolled elation of the whole group – Chii-nii and Fai apart – that he dared not say too much about the way ahead. On the one hand it was all downhill, descending giant step by giant step via great plateaux to sea level, but on the other there was still a lot of ground to cover.

As he confided to Chii-nii, he feared insurrection, rebellion. Never before in his knowledge had Mandarins flown so far, and nerves were fraying. Especially among the newcomers, a few of whom had begun questioning the authority of the Nine in One, and the need to go any further.

Best to let them go into town and let off steam, he decided with a deep sigh. I just hope they stay in the old town and don't stray too far into the suburbs; I hope they don't get into trouble.

What kind of trouble? worried Hu-tu.

Like getting caught and caged or eaten.

WARM WELCOME

Ringed by mountains, Lijiang was remote, inaccessible during the winter months. From spring to autumn, however, there were always a few intrepid foreign backpackers, groups of tourists, and the odd scholarly-looking individual with a book that was not a tourist guide wandering the enchanting streets of the old town.

Swimming in the shade of trailing willows along one of the many small canals that criss-crossed a labyrinth of narrow, stone-paved streets, Lok looked up to see one such man peering down from a small arching bridge at them through metal-rimmed glasses with a look of utter amazement on his not-so-young but not-so-old, lined but sensitive face.

Good heavens, he exclaimed. Mandarins! A whole bevy of you, and all drakes.

The man with a lined but sensitive face and a book about the de-coding of Naxi hieroglyphics closed it and, seeing the ducks were swimming on under the bridge, scuttled along the side of the conduit to keep up.

Wait, he called. Wait. I need to video this for the museum: the day Mandarins came to town. You have no idea how unusual this is, a record in fact.

How ironic, Lok was thinking. Li Qin's big chance and she's not here.

Yes, I am, contradicted a voice behind him, and turning, there she was. No sooner had the thought come and gone than Li Qin was by his side.

My goodness, he remarked, shocked to the core. Are you turning into a mind reader like Chii-nii?

The man with a lined but sensitive face was also surprised, because one moment there were only drakes, and the next a hen appeared as if by magic.

Maybe, replied Li Qin, calm as anything. And that apparently was that. Having charmed her way to the front of the group to swim alongside Lok, she posed for the man with the book (now in his bag) and the camera (out of the bag and purring gently in action like a contented cat).

Such a rare occurrence swiftly drew a crowd. Young and old poured out of brightly painted doorways or leaned out of windows in the lovely old traditional houses, chattering with excitement. They all knew about Mandarins and some had seen pictures, but most had never seen one for real before.

Shall we fraternize with the natives, or stay aloof? wondered Lok. To which the group replied as one: fraternize. And what fun they had!

The noise made by the crowds that gathered – and got larger and larger as everyone followed the ducks as they swam around the centre of town – was terrific, chattering, calling, spitting, munching and crunching ... the Chinese really knew how to have a good time when such an occasion presented itself.

Lok reverted to form, snapping up half-eaten sunflower seeds and anything else edible that came his way. At several points, Li Qin choreographed an off-the-cuff tribal dance she had observed in Myanmar and in doing so showed off her prettily pale plumage to the camera (still purring) for posterity.

Such a lovely sight: snow-capped mountains in the distance. Rice paddies and fields all around. Architecture that had remained largely unchanged for eight centuries.

Tiled rooftops and eaves. Lovely interiors with decorated beams and window frames, some overhanging the canals, with wooden walkways and decks offering all manner of opportunities for small gardens and flowers.

Naxi women still wearing indigo-dyed pleated skirts, some with sheepskin shawls around their shoulders – for the nights were growing cooler – decorated with seven stars and seven ribbons.

As dusk crept in among the houses, red lanterns were lit in alley ways and fans opened to wave away moths and mosquitoes. The party continued until children lay sleeping and dreaming in the arms of relatives. Or curled up like puppies on stone-slabbed or pebbled pathways.

And drunks – young and old – began falling into the water.

A HELPING HAND

Chii-nii was interested to hear the next day that the man with the book and the camera had such a lined face. Was his life so hard? she wondered.

Li Qin explained that he had spent all his life studying the Dongba Scripture and the Naxi language and culture, and was still stuck on certain pictograms as used in the written languages of ancient times.

He is so depressed, she added. Even talking about giving up and going to Chongqing to work in a factory.

Oh we can't have that! exclaimed Chii-nii. Normally I try not to intervene in human affairs, but in this case I think I'll make an exception. I will drop one meaningful hint into his mind and all the rest will follow. This will quickly make him the world authority and soon he will be in great demand to pass on his knowledge.

Why? asked Bo.

Humans have left messages for their descendants over thousands of years. Mostly they are ignored, but there are some individuals who are genuinely interested in knowing what their ancestors were trying to tell them. The Naxi are no different ... as an ethnic minority living here in Yunnan, in Sichuan and Tibet, they have much to teach us.

What about? Bo again.

They believe that everything has spirit and that nothing ever dies. At births and deaths, weddings and seasonal festivals, still a wizard is invited to chant. Dogma-driven religions never ever properly took root. A bit like Japan in that respect.

Now sit to one side while I whip up a spell ...

Li Qin wanted to know about the seven stars and seven ribbons. But had to wait until Chii-nii had completed her good work for the morning.

Seven? Ah, a magnificent mathematical number if ever there was one and always manifesting abundantly in his or her stories. Seven days in a week. The seven hills of Rome. Christianity's seven deadly sins. Canada's painterly Group of Seven. The seven sages of the bamboo grove ...

Sounds Chinese, noted Shuang, who had joined them to listen.

Yes, they were Taoist scholars who centuries ago were critical of authority and stressed personal freedom, spontaneity, strong ale and a celebration of nature.

Sound like great guys to me, a bit like us out on the town yesterday, said Lok. Except for the ale, that is. I really would like to try some; it seems to make humans really happy.

Time to go, interjected Chung. I have spoken with the newcomers and a few – three pairs – wish to stay here on the lake. I suggest we give them our blessing and let them go. If they can start a colony in Lijiang, I think that would be wonderful, don't you?

After a short discussion it was agreed, and the remainder pressed on.

END OF THE WORLD?

As they flew across country, there was the faint echo of a terrible sound far to the north, remnants of a blinding incandescence, and they thought they saw something white and shining fly up into the sky.

What? they cried, diving for safety, for all but Chung, Fai and Chii-nii felt very afraid.

A rocket test from the Xichang Space Station, she explained. Even Chinese humans are exploring the sky.

Why bother when they can't even make life on Earth work properly? Dewei observed cynically.

I'm afraid that may be the point, replied Chung sadly. Having exploited and messed up their home to the point of catastrophe, humankind may soon need to migrate to the stars.

TRIALS AND TRIBULATIONS

Having alighted on Dashanbao wetlands outside the city of Zhaotong, Cong was circling Chii-nii. So was Dewei!

Shuang watched his older brothers with some amusement. No chance, he thought. No chance at all.

Hu-tu was busy re-evaluating the mating potential of the remaining male ducks that had joined them in Turkmenistan.

Bo was wishing she could be with Fai, while knowing in her heart of hearts that any interest in that direction would not be reciprocated.

Chung was paddling with the widow, and wishing in foolish moments he was five years younger. But neither was seriously attentive; they just liked one another.

As for Fai, he kept his head down and stayed in a world of his own. With luck, any onlooker would simply think him a piece of foam, or some crumpled paper refuse. At worst they would throw stones to try and sink him. At best, he thought, they might succeed.

Not that the newly arrived Black-necked cranes were much bothered by the worries of others. They were too busy recovering from their own migration and settling in for the winter.

They certainly were not interested in the difficulties of the city, experiencing long-term drought and a mass exodus of people of working age to the east. All around farmers were struggling to keep fields irrigated; in Zhaotong, parents were trying to persuade their children to stay home.

To prevent them from migrating.

PRETTY HISTORIC

Zunyi, a city in a province of seven million in North Guizhou, and as Lok observed, who had ever heard of it? Situated on the Xiangliang River but with no rainfall since August, the convoy steered clear and rested instead in Chishui, a resort of waterfalls, enormous stands of bamboo, horse chestnut trees, a pretty lake named Ever Bright Moonlight, and a famous historic landmark.

Once upon a time, began Chung, smiling benignly, there was a man named Mao Zedong ...

As a young man Mao was an avowed communist who pledged to rid the country of its dynastic feudal system and feed the whole of China. Sadly he lost his way, caused as much harm as good, and over the years became what he had set out to replace: a self-serving dictator.

In January 1935, he arrived in Zunyi at the head of his Red Army on the famed Long March to Beijing. That was when everyone was fired up with enthusiasm for change. A conference was held in a building on the Hongqi Road, now a designated cultural relic.

Not interested, stated Hu-tu, itching to get home. Where next?

Yuanling. Changde. Then across the water to Yueyang. Believe me, dear children, we are nearly there.

PEKING DUCK

It was Bo who first dared to ask about the millions of white ducks they saw being herded and harried all over China.

Watching them dashing about in paddy fields, chasing frogs and eating weeds to help keep the young rice growing clean and healthy was one thing. Seeing them penned in great enclosures with hardly room to move was another.

They're not wild ducks. They're nothing like us, being twice our size. So why do humans keep so many? Do they ...

She halted here, for fear of learning the truth ...

Do they, eat them?

Chung nodded. They are bred for meat and eggs, he said. Also feathers and down ... little is wasted. There are thousands of ways to cook and present them, duck being the third most popular meat after pork and chicken. But perhaps the most famous internationally is Peking Duck.

It was weird to hear of your kind being described in such a way. It made Hu-tu feel quite weak. As for Lok, he was torn between empathy and epicurean curiosity.

Shall I go on? asked Chung. This is the reality of China. Best to look it in the face and be unafraid of fear. A bit like looking death in the face, the only way to understand that ultimately it is nothing.

Many of the ducks were not sure that death was nothing. But they were happy to rock back on their webbed feet and listen:

Peking Duck originated in Nanjing. They were small black ducks that fed on grain spilled from barges on canals linking the waterways and not only grew fat but also started developing white feathers. That was when humans began domesticating them.

Really? Bo looked startled, and wondered if Fai was listening.

Nowadays the ducklings live naturally for around six weeks but are then force-fed four times a day until they are fat enough for eating.

Force-fed? That's disgusting, said Shuang.

And cruel, added Cong.

Lok was quiet and still.

The ducks are then killed, de-feathered, their innards torn out and rinsed through with water.

Bo's eyes were out on stalks.

Air is pumped under the skin to separate the fat, the duck is boiled and then hung up to dry. While hanging it is glazed with a sweet malt syrup, then after hanging for a day, roasted in an oven until shiny brown. If you go into cities, towns or villages, you will see them hanging outside restaurants everywhere.

Lok felt truly ashamed.

Hu-tu felt sick.

Shuang wanted to release all the ducks into the wild.

Cong thought he'd help, starting immediately.

Dewei wondered if there was a law relating to the treatment of ducks in China.

They all – including Chii-nii and Li Qin – clung together, thoroughly disturbed.

We are so blessed, Chii-nii said quietly. We are so blessed to taste bad to humans.

Li Qin agreed, saying she would never ever complain about anything ever again. And then voiced a beautiful and solemn prayer for all ducks destined for the table that had them all in tears.

Lok was so proud he forgot all about addictively programmed hunger pains. When his mate was silly, she was very, very silly, but when she was impressive, she was truly, truly impressive. He knew which side of her character he liked and admired more.

JUST A DAY AWAY

The flight across Dongting Lake to Yueyang was made eventful only by a flock of geese heading ever southwards.

Why are you going north? the leader queried in midair – a risky undertaking in itself.

We are heading for Yuanyang Lake. Do you know it?

Oh yes, there are thousands of ducks like you there. I guess that's why it's known as Mandarin Duck Lake. You're only a day or so away now. Good luck.

That night, resting on the lakeside, Cong asked Chung how he had known about Yuanyang. There were so many lakes with beautiful names all over China: Heavenly Lake (once called Jade Lake) in Tianchi. Crescent Lake, near Dunhuang in the desert to the far north. The human-made One Hundred Flower Pond, right in the heart of Jinan, in Shandong.

Chung was pleased that Cong knew so much already. A worthy student. As to Lok, while very bright and knowledgeable, he was himself the first to admit that he was too open to distraction. Maybe Cong and his son could work together to carry them all into the future.

When Chung passed on ...

FIRST SIGHTING

The flock flew slowly now, as if understanding on some deep level that they might never need to fly any serious distance again. Their wings beat as one; their hearts were as one.

All except Chii-nii and Fai, who knew that their own journey was incomplete.

But as they all descended towards Yuanyang, the flock was flying as if in slow motion, tired beyond measure and yet determined to savour every last second of the experience.

Splash!

That was Cong, of course, unintentionally but as always in the lead.

Splash, splash, splash ...

Chung, Lok and Li Qin.

Splash, splash, splash splash …
Dewei, Shuang, Hu-tu and Bo.
Splash, splash, splash ...
Chii-nii, Fai and the widow, Xiao Chen.
Then the survivors of the shadow group of nine, followed by all the others ...
They had arrived.
But arrived where exactly? And what now?

WUYUAN

There are in fact two major lakes in China named after our kind, Chung explained. The one in Jiaxing is thought by humans to resemble the shape of a Mandarin, and it is a pleasant place, I have been told. But it is close to the sea and halfway between two massive cities, Shanghai to the north and Hangzhou.

I believe this the better location. We are in the mountains. Secluded. And though many tourists come to Wuyuan, we are in a traditional world that retains much of its charm and simpler slower ways of life.

Lok and Li Qin were not sure. Might they not get bored?

Stay the winter, Chung pleaded. Give this place a chance. See how you feel in spring.

Hu-tu and Bo were already making themselves feel at home, paddling this way and that and amazed at the number of northern Mandarins doing exactly the same.

What is a stranger but a friend not met yet? Bo decided, and with a new bravado and Hu-tu in tow, paddled off to introduce herself.

Yuanyang Lake is the largest winter habitat of wild Mandarins in Asia, maybe the world, Chung continued.

Are we wild? wondered Cong.

I believe we are both wild and free and the friend of good human beings, Chung replied. I suppose that makes us semi-wild and semi-domesticated. In spring, you can decide on which side of the fence you choose to sit, and either stay here all the year round, or join others in heading north for the summer.

Or head west, back to Europe, suggested Lok. I do miss the food.

I thought, said a small quiet voice, that this trip was all about coming home.

It was Shuang, the home boy, who reminded them all of why they had come in the first place.

This triggered a long discussion on the definition of the word. What home meant to each of them, one by one.

For Lok it meant being with Li Qin, and vice versa.

For Bo it meant feeling safe and a quiet easy life.

For Shuang it meant staying close to family and friends and the sense of security they provided.

For Cong, it meant being in a place that offered the opportunity to grow.

For Dewei it meant peace and quiet, and the laws of structure and conformity.

For Hu-tu, it meant family and caring for others.

And Chung … Chung, who had made his dream come true … to come home … finally felt at one with his roots, and was ready to join his ancestors.

For Chii-nii, it was all of these things, and none at all. For a goddess lived everywhere and nowhere … Now she was here, but tomorrow?

SETTLING IN

We are in a marvellous area, Chung observed to anyone within listening distance. In the west of Wuyuan country, surrounded by mountains that in many places sweep right down to the water's edge. Believe it or not, this lake was originally a reservoir called Datang Dock, but the environment proved so healthy and protected that wildlife quickly took over.

The scenery in and around Wuyuan is quite spectacular, he continued. Many say that even agriculturally it is the most beautiful countryside in all China. And as for the towns, they are to this part of the world in Jiangxi Province, as Lijiang was to Yunnan Province: well preserved and full of life and interest. Now why are you all laughing?

Because you sound like a tourist guide, giggled Bo. She was perched on a branch overhanging the water and preening her feathers. Fed, watered, with her siblings and adopted family around her, she could not imagine feeling happier.

There are some wonderful trees around here, full of holes for nesting, remarked Hu-tu. Many are used year after year by the same pairs, but there are plenty more that are just asking for a clutch of eggs and a happy brood of ducklings to go fly.

I think this may be Shangri-la, added Bo. Paradise.

There were many sounds that night as they slept fitfully ... in yet another new place, but they were also excited that it might be their final resting place.

Breezes whisked through leaves and levered more than a few from their branches to fall fluttering to the ground or ruffling the surface of the water. Autumn. The sound of nocturnal animals on the move, preparing for winter ... Insects still vibrating, but ever more quietly and slowly ...

TO THE RESCUE

As Chii-nii announced the next morning, she and Fai had shared a dream: to make one more trip.

Chung sighed.

Until now he had thought that he alone knew that there had been a catastrophic disturbance on Japan's largest island of Honshu. First a powerful earthquake, followed a monumental tsunami that had not only swept away towns and cities but so overwhelmed a nuclear facility that many feared the resulting meltdowns and effects of radiation would prove to be infinitely worse than Chernobyl.

We have decided to fly on to Japan and plead our case with as many Mandarins as we can find before the first snowfall. I have the language skills and the magic; Fai hopes that his appearance and situation will be enough to sway any arguments, convince them to come.

The others were quiet. Holding their breath. No one moved.

When were you thinking of leaving? asked Chung, even though he already knew the answer.

We are going now, replied Chii-nii and took off with Fai close on her heels.

See you in a week or so, she called. By the end of the month for sure ...

And for the first time they heard Fai's voice as an affirming echo on the lake.

Goodbye.

Japan

The memories of lost love gather like drifting snow, poignant as the mandarin ducks who float side by side in sleep.

Lady Murasaki

Chihi-nii and Fai flew fast and hard to the east to cross the coast south of Shanghai. It was not hard, she with her special powers, he with his supermandarin own.

But neither had expected to be caught up in a typhoon meandering up from The Philippines. It was trying to decide whether to head for the Korean island of Cheju, or the southern tip of Kyushu, Japan's third largest island after Honshu and Hokkaido to the far north.

This is a bit tougher than I expected, Chii-nii voiced into the squalling wind and driving rain. She and Fai were hanging on for dear life to the mast of a fishing boat that was being tossed around like a speck of duck down rather than several tons of wood and metal.

Shall I work some magic and get us out of this?

Fai declined. As soon as they were in the eye, he would lead and she could follow in his slipstream. In this way they could get ahead and beat the typhoon to its destination. Which was to be ...

Cheju, screamed the wind. Out of my way ...

You know, said Chii-nii, as they landed in Kagoshima to take stock. I think we can truly say we have now flown through every climatic extravagance nature could throw our way: showers, fog, dry heat, humidity, storms, mist, monsoon and now a typhoon. I think the only thing we have not experienced is a lightning strike.

Whereupon the Shinto gods intervened and sent a lightning bolt to strike a boulder beside which they were resting, and shattered it into a million pieces.

My goodness, reacted Chii-nii. Well, it's easy to know who's in charge around here.

And they then watched in amazement as the mountain above exploded and began showering rocks and ash over the slopes below.

Add volcanoes to that list, she screeched, taking to the air for safety. I know it's nothing to do with climate, but it is a supernatural phenomenon.

Fai followed and together they began sending out the word duckepathically. There were thousands of Mandarins somewhere on the archipeligo, but where exactly both were unsure.

Maybe twittering is the answer, Chii-nii relayed to her associate.

Twitter it is, replied Fai. And commenced a little magic of his own.

BIWA-KO

There was quite a crowd when they landed on the banks of Lake Biwa, near Kyoto.

They were very concerned, a strong female spokesduck said. There were so many nuclear reactors located close by the lake. Right now they were idling in response to the disaster in Fukushima, but if humans switched them back on in order to keep warm through the winter, another accident could contaminate the freshwater of forty million Japanese humans and poison the region for the foreseeable future.

We would like to relocate, but preferably in Japan. We don't want to leave our home, especially in such troubled times.

Chii-nii promised to keep a look out for safer waters and let them know. In the meantime, if there were any ducks who fancied moving abroad, at least for a while, they would be more than welcome in Yuanyuang.

She and Fai left them all – male and female, young and old – with a lot to think about. No decision was easy.

KANTO

There were Mandarins on the lotus ponds at the Hachimangu Shrine in Kamakura.

A larger community on Inokashira Pond in the west of Tokyo.

Several in the very heart of the city, at Meiji Jingu Shrine, and a pair testing the waters of the moat around the Imperial Palace.

They all listened. They all argued the advantages and disadvantages. Mostly they seemed very confused, anxious and unsure about what or who to believe.

We are told everything is safe, but it doesn't feel safe, said one female.

We are told Japan is recovering, but how can it when the reactors remain unstable and no-one knows how to repair them or deal with the consequences? said another.

Many of the hens were worried about food resources and breeding the following spring.

All Chii-nii could do was listen, comfort, encourage and offer refuge in China.

China, some of the older Mandarins shivered. They remembered stories ... And wasn't China following in the footsteps of all the other so-called developed countries and by doing so putting itself equally at risk?

Fai was thinking.

How could he make the human race wake up? If an earthquake, tsunami and the meltdown of three, maybe even four reactors would not do it, what would?

Chii-nii heard him but had no solution. Gods and goddesses could watch and laugh and cry and help in small ways on a one-to-one basis, but they did not intervene with human development on the karmic path to enlightenment. It was painful to watch, but surely changing fate was not their job.

But Fai was not a god. He was simply a white Mandarin with certain mutant powers. How could he best use them? he was wondering on the wing.

They both flew north as far as Sendai and then parted.

Chii-nii continued her flight path to Hokkaido, thinking she'd find Mandarins there. But the snow had come early and most had migrated south. Where to? She had no idea.

It did not take long to turn around and return to where she had left Fai, but he had long paddled down the Hirose River and various tributaries towards the coast and the Pacific Ocean.

Fai, where are you? she voiced in desperation. But this time there was no reply.

DAIICHI NO. 4

Fai could not believe the wastelands that lay before him. Mile upon mile of ruination and despoilment ... shattered buildings and lives, poisoned soil and forests. And not so long before it had all been so indescribably beautiful. One of the most beautiful coastlines in the world.

Of course, in years to come, such places would be green and alive again with creatures like himself made strong by long-term exposure to radioactivity. But humans ... what could they do? How could they adapt to survive?

Soon he was over Fukushima and could smell the poison on the wind, sense its potential for harm and danger.

He saw a woman digging for the body of her son around where her house had stood, still missing after a year.

He saw a man trying to construct a house out of debris.

He saw a small group of humans in white suits inside a danger zone laying flowers.

One young man had seen his wife swept away, carrying their unborn child.

A girl had clung to a rooftop with her parents and on their insistence swum away rather than drown with them.

A small child had lost his entire family of four generations.

Soon Fai was over the Daiichi plant and felt nearly overwhelmed by the extent of the damage and his sense of foreboding. The first reactor was hidden inside a box-like structure, and workers were struggling in suits, boots and gloves, masks and helmets to cover the other two. But the fourth, said to be close to collapse, was open to the sky.

He could see right down into the pool of water, the hundreds of fuel rods just sitting there, waiting ...

My mission! he realised. Accepted.

And without a second's hesitation, his pure white plumage incandescent, flashing all the colours of the rainbow, he dove down into the incipient catastrophe below.

SECOND CHANCE

All Japan saw the blinding light and feared the worst.

People fell to their knees and prayed as never before.

But then came reports that instruments were indicating that fuel rods were rendered safe and meltdowns inactive. No reactor would switch on; geiger counters registered zero on nuclear waste.

Politicians forgot why they had ordered the reactors to be built in the first place and took up hobbies and pilgrimages.

Corporate interests and the stock market handed back their ill-gotten gains and volunteered to clean up and start small, ecologically sound businesses in the stricken areas.

Everyone acknowledged that to be given a second chance was miraculous and, while vowing to do better, wondered how and why it had come about.

If we blindly follow a second time around, they agreed, then we really do deserve to fail as an intelligent life form.

It truly was the chance for a new beginning.

China (again)

There is one order of beauty which seems made to turn heads. It is a beauty like that of kittens, or very small downy ducks making gentle rippling noises with their soft bills, or babies just beginning to toddle.
George Eliot (Adam Bede)

It was late November when Chii-nii returned.

First she had to explain why Fai was not with her, and though she did not know the details, she had felt his energy rush through her as he made the ultimate sacrifice.

He gave himself to save us all, she concluded, sad but already planning a new piece of weaving in Fai's memory: the net of all nets that saved the world.

It was easier to explain why she did not have a single Mandarin in tow.

They don't need to leave home now, she explained. Like the humans, they are concentrating their efforts on making the places where they live as healthy and bio-dynamically productive as possible. They are taking responsibility.

The Group of Nine remained close, but all the other Mandarins had dispersed around the lake.

Cong had accepted that Chii-nii was too busy and connected to be concerned with a single relationship. He was welcoming a new sense of peace and calm within. Learning to compromise.

Dewei was understanding that the middle path was more rewarding than right or wrong. Instead of judging Xiao Chen, he was seeing the qualities that Chung had recognized. He was still making mental lists, but less and less frequently.

Shuang was finding that he had enough natural reserves of energy and intellect to carry his life forward without sinking into self-doubt or panic. He was still loyal and lovely, but also determined in his confidence.

Hu-tu was realizing that love was not conditional. That she was not indispensable. That her need to look after others was no more than a reflection of her pain – a body of pain that she shared in one form or another with all her siblings – at having been abandoned so early.

Bo was accepting that the discomforting nature of change was a natural part of life. She realized that her passive-aggression was triggered by a fear of being found wanting and discounted.

Lok was learning to do one thing at a time and not be so easily distracted. It was a surprise to discover that the negative had as much to offer as the positive, and that with will power and clarity addictions could be resolved.

Li Qin was moderating her pace, accepting that love comes from being, not doing and having. Also she was practising asking herself what really mattered and being more patient.

Chii-nii was grounded, appreciating the everyday. She had always known that she was interconnected with all life; that is why she wove with such intensity of emotion. Now she could continue her life work in peace and calm.

As for Chung, taking on the role of teacher and sage had countered a tendency to withhold his emotions and retreating into his mind.

Now he knew – the journey having proved it once and for all – that there was an ample supply of knowledge and energy for everyone's needs.

Beautifully in balance, and with a great sense of fulfillment and happiness to be home, he watched his family, as he liked to call them all, settling for the night.

It was a beautiful golden evening. The shadows around the lakeside pooled deep indigo, purple, lilac and green.

He felt a sudden tiredness and then a detachment, as if something was leaving his body.

Looking across the lake, he saw his mate beckoning, walking – or rather waddling – on water.

RENEWAL

After months of quiet, the lake was seething with activity. Many of the Mandarins from the north had left for their summer haunts, but eight of the Group of Nine, their shadow counterparts and many of the others who had flown with them had paired off and nested.

Li Qin had decided to try her webbed feet at motherhood and Lok seemed content enough.

Cong and Shuang, having bowed to Chii-nii's greater talents as a goddess, had both found intelligent, loyal mates that Chung would surely have approved of.

After a heart-to-heart one day, Dewei and Xiao Chen decided to give love a chance and were soon inseparable.

Hu-tu and Bo had no trouble at all in attracting partners. In fact, there was quite a fight over both of them, though more in rumbling mode than serious battle.

Every full moon, they met together to remember Chung and reminisce: Scotland, England, the North Sea and ever onwards into Europe, the Middle East and Asia. So many adventures ...

We need to be word perfect in order to pass the stories on, decreed Chii-nii, already an aunt to more than a few ...

She had that very morning watched Bo's brood – twelve perfect fluff-ball ducklings – launch into the air from a hole in a tree twenty feet off the ground, each landing in a flurry of leaves from the old year.

Such joy! she thought, and then took a break from weaving to hone her skills at two new hobbies: reading raindrops and rainbow gazing.

FIVE FEATHERS

One clear day, she witnessed in recall – as if in a crystal – Chung shedding white down in the reservoir in Shropshire, and saw it begin to flower ...

Another day, during a cool shower, she saw a blue feather fall into the sea and somehow seek out Fai, urging him to join them. En route oceans were purged of all pollution, and where it eventually came to rest in the Ukraine, a source of pure water sprang where no water had been safe for decades.

Water became clean.

One windy day she saw a black tail feather being chased by a flock of Mandarins. Once overtaken, it conducted the passage of a tornado so as to avoid storks nesting on rooftops, and helped an eagle through some turbulence.

Air became clean.

One morning she saw a green feather left among trees and leaves move to reforest every continent to raise oxygen levels and revive all living things.

Nature became healthy.

Soon after she saw two small subtle-toned feathers fall onto land, marking and clearing the way to repairing the damage of centuries. And later, a scattering of more, with a hint of green, to further help bring mountains tops and valleys into harmony.

Earth became clean.

As to who dropped purple, red and orange feathers as they flew? No matter.

Fire became cleansing.

Most magical and life-changing of all, Chi-nii saw multi-coloured Mandarin feathers dancing all around the planet, up into the aether and far down into the bowels of the earth.

When Gaia – our one and only beloved mother – woke that perfect spring, everything was cleansed and renewed. The world could start again.

*****

The very idea of a bird is a symbol and a suggestion to the poet. A bird seems to be at the top of the scale, so vehement and intense his life ... The beautiful vagabonds, endowed with every grace, masters of all climes, and knowing no bounds – how many human aspirations are realised in their free, holiday-lives – and how many suggestions to the poet in their flight and song!

John Burroughs

Acknowledgements

As usual, the creation of this book has been an international effort.

Paul and Ena Latham in Perthshire, Scotland, whose experience inspired the idea for the story.

A huge debt of gratitude to Sir Christopher Lever, the Hon. Life President of TUSK and a lifelong supporter and enthusiast of the natural world, who so kindly and generously read the manuscript for ornithological accuracy. His own book, The Mandarin Duck, published by T&A Poyser in 2013, is the iconic academic authority.

Love to psychotherapist Azzah Manukova in Mexico, who in introducing me to The Enneagram in 2001, helped me turn my life around. Also the Chilean pysychiatrist and writer Claudio Naranjo (1932-2019), a principal developer in Enneagram of Personality Theories, whom I was privileged to meet for breakfast and to interview for The Japan Times in Tokyo in 2010:

*https://www.enneagraminstitute.com/the-traditional-enneagram.

*https://en.wikipedia.org/wiki/Enneagram_of_Personality

Respect to Rajah Banerjee who founded the one and only biodynamic tea estate in India's West Bengal. He retired in 2018. Meeting him in Tokyo in the 1990s, I learned he had heard about

Rudolf Steiner's biodynamic farming philosophy from British authority David Clements at a conference in Berlin. David (also a violinist) and my mother (cellist) used to play in a quartet together in the 1930s. And so the world turns …

Hugs to George Bussey in Florida, USA, Jacinta Hin in Tokyo, Japan, Marian Duffy in Meigle and Wendy Birse in Balbeggie, Scotand, who read, enthused (while pointing out anomolies), and pushed me on to publish …

Appreciation as always to Jillian Yorke in New Zealand for proof-reading and editing.

A grateful nod to Andy Melia in Liverpool for copy-writing advice.

Admiration and respect for illustrator Meilo So on Yell, Shetland, Scotland, for her beautiful artwork.

Near last but not least, the hugely talented and forever patient Alan White, recently moved back to the UK from Alberta, Canada for layout and design. Another fine job, Al.

Finally, more than a few blown kisses across the garden at Burnside to Akii (Yasuyuki Ueda), contained in his own workspace, for continuing support and encouragement.

Sources

Respect to all those, living, dead, unknown, famous and infamous, whose lines and verses I have quoted to introduce each chapter. Legal permissions are a difficult field to negotiate for independents, but all copyrights fully acknowledged, respected and appreciated:

Page i **Jerome David Salinger** (1921-2010) Lines generally interpreted as symbolizing the curiosity of youth. Originally published in the USA in serial form in the 1940s, as a novel in 1951.

Page 1 **Rabbie/Robbie Burns** (1759-1796) Writing on universal themes of love and nature, nowadays widely regarded as Scotland's national poet.

Page 17 **Kenneth Grahame** (1859-1932) Scottish writer best known for the children's novel, The Wind in the Willows, published by 1908.

Page 67 **Carl Sagan** (1934-1996) American astronomer, astrophysicist and science communicator who wrote 80 books: the Brian Cox of his day.

Page 71 **Bill Murphy** (1950-) American actor, comedian, artist and writer; known for a deadpan delivery.

Page 79 **Richard P. Feynman** (1918-1988) American confronter of conventional wisdom; Nobel Prize-winning quantum physicist.

Page 83 **Michael Leunig** (1945-) Australian cartoonist and painter, writer, philosopher and poet.

Page 103 **Katherine Patterson** (1932-) American-Chinese author of some 30 books; mainly childrens' novels.

Page 111 **Farid Al-Din Attar** Persian-born Sufi poet and mystic in the latter half of the 12th century. His most renowned work, the Conference of Birds, concerns the difficult journey to enlightenment, and the excuses we make to avoid even setting out.

Page 117 **Enid Bagnold** (1889-1981) British author (National Velvet) and playwright. (Described by Virginia Woolf as "a scallywag who married a very rich man.")

Page 121 **Victor Marie Hugo** (1802-1885) French poet, dramatist and novelist; leader of the Romantic Movement.

Page 129 **Bikash Bista** (1976-) left Nepal to live in New York in 2008, when the Nepali community was growing fast. The line quoted is from a poem read at a poetry festival, saying such events helped him maintain a connection with his native land.

Page 131 **Douglas Jerrold** (1803-1857) English journalist, writer, dramatist; reputed to be a great conversational wit.

Page 141 **Scott Weidensaul** (1959-) Pennsylvania-based American naturalist and author of 38 titles, who claims to live books rather than write them.

Page 161 **Lady Murasaki/Murasaki Shikibu** (c.978-c.1014) Japanese writer and lady-in-waiting in the Heian Period Imperial court in Kyoto; author of Genji monogatari (The Tale of Genji), regarded as the world's first full-length novel.

Page 167 **George Eliot/Mary Ann Evans** (1819-1880) Novelist, poet, journalist and translator; a leading literary figure in Victorian England.

Page 171 **John Burroughs** (1837-1921) American naturalist, nature essayist and gardener; a pioneer in US conservation.

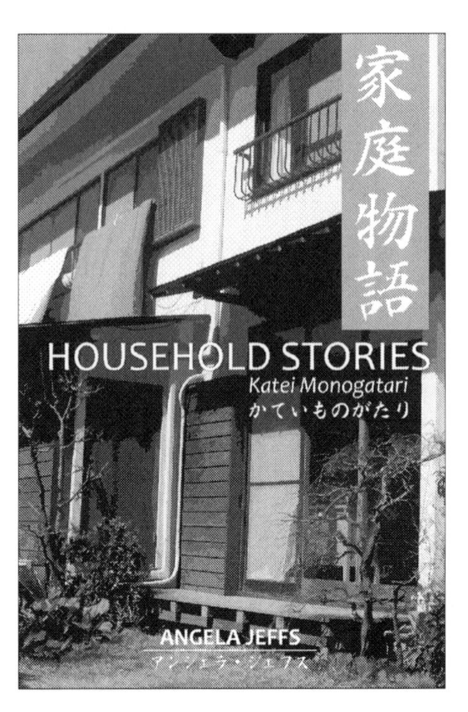

ALSO BY THE AUTHOR

Have you read ***Household Stories/ Katei Monogatari*** (which means household stories in Japanese)?

Written in Japan between 2010-2012, this book was published in late 2017 after the author moved to Scotland.

"A love story with a difference", it describes in intricate and loving detail an intense relationship between the author and the house she lived in in Japan for over a decade. Moving from inside to outside and from room to room, she leads the reader on a fascinating and increasingly urgent journey through the interior, and the life lived within its four walls.

Why did she feel so driven? As she wrote during the traumatic months following on from the earthquake, tsunami and nuclear meltdowns of March 2011: "Because we may not be here much longer, and even if we stay here, life is shifting, the world in transition, and I want to remember. Remember it all."

What readers say about ***Household Stories/Katei Monogatari***:

Kathleen Kimball-Baker (13 May 2015) – verified Amazon purchase in US
***** *Charming and disarming!*
"Reading "Household Stories" gave me the crash-course in Japanese customs, language, landscape, ecology, manners, spirituality, architecture, transportation, cities, and countryside that I've been seeking. I'm not so afraid now to consider a visit there!"

C Watson (6 December 2017) – verified Amazon purchase in UK
***** *Fascinating.*
"Started reading it with my lunch one day, and didn't want to stop."

B'dette (9 May 2018) – verified Amazon purchase in Japan
***** *Room by room*
"A wonderful journey."

Amazon customer (15 June 2018)
"She writes so lovingly of possessions and objects, their history and how they became part of the house ... It is a 'love story', and has made me look at my house in a completely different way."

Nancy Walker (3 August 2018) – verified Amazon purchase in US
***** *Rooms of a Japanese experience*
"A must for someone who wants to experience Japan through words. I want to get on the next plane."

Bunkajin (5 March 2019) – verified Amazon purchase in Japan
***** *A home and a life, from the inside out*
"My father's house has many rooms," the Bible quotes Jesus as saying. So did Angela's, and some of them bordered on the divine."

C Hannan (15 May 2019) – verified Amazon purchase
"Love this book. I was right there, with her."

E.A. Hodgson (19 June 2019) – verified Amazon purchase in UK
***** "Having found it hard to put down, I rationed reading in small sections to delay finishing."

Crystal (14 February 2018) – posted on Goodreads
**** "A memoir that uses the rooms of a house and the things they hold to reveal the stories of the author's life could be a bit precious in the wrong hands, but this book strikes just the right tone, and I looked forward to visiting each new room every morning on my commute."

Also by Angela Jeffs

Published in 2013, after ten years in the writing, this is far more than a month-long travelogue. A mix of memoir, adventure, self-help and survival, it is a roller-coaster of emotions, an intriguing family history, and a sometimes painful personal memoir. Based on a journey made to South America in 1999, it links three continents, five countries, and one hundred and seven letters written by the author's paternal grandfather in Buenos Aires to her father in England between the early 1930s and 1954. It is a true labour of love to find a far-flung family from the distant and not-so-distant past.

"My grandfather described the events of his life in Argentina and Uruguay, after his wife in Liverpool cast him out, as 'a mad romp'. Believe me, the trip I made – with no Spanish and little to no idea what I was going to do when I got there – beats his own hands down! But what an amazing learning curve ..."

What readers say about *Chasing Shooting Stars*:

Single Dad (5 March 2013) – verified Amazon purchase in UK
***** ***Phew! I'm emotionally drained***
"An incredible book by an incredible storyteller."

Gaucho (5 March 2013) – verified Amazon purchase
***** *In Argentina*
"For years I've had a guide book to Buenos Aires on my bookshelf but come to realize I'm never going to get there. Now Angela Jeffs has made the journey for me … and intriguingly I'm only a third of the way through – there's more to come!"

Amazon customer Mike (5 October 2015) – verified Amazon purchase in EU
***** *A must read*
"It's totally gripping and not a little painful and very well written. What a brave thing to have done, both to make the journey and to write the book."

Liane Wakayabashi (4 November 2015) – verified Amazon purchase in Japan
***** *A family saga taking place on three continents*
"I loved Chasing Shooting Stars! Maybe it's because I share Angela Jeffs' yearning to know about ancestors who crossed oceans to create lives so far from where we were born. When the author journeys more than halfway around the world from Japan to Argentina in hopes of discovering the roots of a family she shared only in name, she discovers that they are waiting with open arms for her – whether she likes it or not!"

Jacinta Hin (6 April 2013) – posted on Goodreads
"A wonderful and beautifully written book full of wit and unexpected turns … Once you start reading, you will not be able to put it down!"